English Wits and Riddles
英文奇言妙語

齊玉 編著　毛治平 繪

Cellar

Q: How can a cat go into a cellar with four feet and come out with eight?

國家圖書館出版品預行編目資料

英文奇言妙語 English Wits and Riddles / 齊玉編著;毛
治平插畫. －－增訂二版二刷. －－臺北市: 三民,
2011
　　面; 公分

ISBN 978–957–14–5358–3 （平裝）
1. 英語 2. 讀本

805.18　　　　　　　　　　　　　　　99012418

© 　英文奇言妙語 English Wits and Riddles

編 著 者	齊　玉
插畫設計	毛治平
責任編輯	陳逸如
美術設計	吳立新

發 行 人	劉振強
著作財產權人	三民書局股份有限公司
發 行 所	三民書局股份有限公司
	地址　臺北市復興北路386號
	電話　(02)25006600
	郵撥帳號　0009998–5
門 市 部	(復北店) 臺北市復興北路386號
	(重南店) 臺北市重慶南路一段61號

出版日期	初版一刷　2009年4月
	增訂二版一刷　2010年10月
	增訂二版二刷　2011年2月
編　　號	S 807820

行政院新聞局登記證局版臺業字第○二○○號

有著作權‧不准侵害

ISBN　978–957–14–5358–3　（平裝）

http://www.sanmin.com.tw　三民網路書店
※本書如有缺頁、破損或裝訂錯誤，請寄回本公司更換。

序

　　本書內容包括謎語 (riddle) 和名言佳句奇文。有一個中文謎題頗饒思索：「園中花，化成灰，夕陽一點已西墜。相思淚，心已碎，空轉馬蹄歸。秋紅已殘，螢火已飛。」猜百家姓之一。謎底是「蘇」。英文也有很多不同類型的謎語，值得推敲思考。例如：What is worse than finding a worm in an apple?（什麼比在蘋果裡發現一條蟲更糟？）答案不是「很多條蟲。」而是 Finding half a worm.（發現半條蟲。）因為發現半條蟲時，另一半早已下肚，當然比發現一條蟲更糟。又例如：Which can move faster, heat or cold?（何者移動較快，熱或冷？）謎底是 "heat"。因為 You can catch cold.（你能捉到冷／你會感冒。）另有押韻的謎題：A houseful, a roomful, can't catch a spoonful. What is it?（滿屋子，滿房間，卻裝不滿一湯匙，是什麼？）謎底是 "smoke"（煙）。

　　常讀謎語、名言和佳句，不但能啟發機智，增加智慧，激發邏輯思考力和想像力，更可充實字彙，強化文法，進而提高英文的水平，對一般讀者、英文教師和學生們都有莫大的助益。

　　英文廿六個字母的排列組合變化多端，可建構出巧妙的單字、片語、句子和短文。其中有同義詞 (synonym)，反義詞 (antonym)，變位字 (anagram)。例如：listen 和 silent 二字的字母全同，但排列位置不同。還有回文 (palindrome)。例如：You can cage a swallow, can't you? But you can't swallow a cage, can you?（你能把燕子關在籠子裡，不是嗎？但你不能嚥下籠子，是嗎？）這句話不管是順著唸或倒著唸都一樣。

　　《英文奇言妙語》乃根據昔日作者與先叔毛建漢合著而現已絕版之《益智英文》重新編寫而成。除了謎題以外，還有單字片語和編者額外的補充，讓讀者能更詳盡的了解書中的謎語。本書中的插畫為編者長子毛治平（《毛毛歷險記》、《有男生愛女生》、《校園阿肯》等書作者）所繪；另請三子毛振平（臺大外文系畢業。現任台南市大必佳美語補習班負責人）擔任校正工作。本書英文書名 *English Wits and Riddles* 中 "wits" 一字乃採作者昔日初中（即今國中）、高中同窗六年的李清木君（民國四十八年全國大專聯考狀元）之建議而得，謹此申謝。

編者謹識

English 英文奇言妙語
Wits and Riddles

Contents 目 次

English 英文奇言妙語
Wits and Riddles

① *Who*

6W1H 的第一個字是 Who。Who 的用法很多,除用作疑問詞之外,尚可作關係代名詞之用。例如:

◇ **Who in the world did it?**(究竟是誰做了這件事?)

→ in the world 可作「到底」,「究竟」解,用以加強 who, what, how 等字的意思。這句的 who 是作疑問詞之用。

◇ **He who knows not and knows not he knows not, is dangerous, shun him.**

(其人不知而不知其不知,危矣,避之。)

He who knows not and knows he knows not, is simple, teach him.

(其人不知而知其不知,憨矣,教之。)

He who knows and knows not he knows, is sleeping, wake him.

(其人知而不知其知,昏矣,喚之。)

He who knows and knows he knows, is wise, follow him.

(其人知而知其知,智矣,法之。)

→ 四句中的 who 作關係代名詞之用。

◇ **He who humbles himself will be made great.**(自謙者人必尊之。)

He who makes himself great will be humbled.(自大者人必貶之。)

→ 這兩句中的 who 也是關係代名詞。

◇ **Who can help the many who are poor?**(誰能幫助貧窮的多數人?)

Who can save the few who are rich?(誰能拯救富有的少數人?)

→ 上兩句中第一個 who 是疑問詞,第二個 who 是關係代名詞。the many(多數人),the few(少數人)。many 和 few 是形容詞,形容詞前加定冠詞 the 就成了複數形的名詞。

◇ **Anyone who hears my teachings and obeys them is like a wise man who** builds his house on solid rock.（任何一個聽到我的教誨並遵照著做的人就像一個聰明的人，他將房子建在堅硬的岩石上。）

Anyone who hears my teachings but does not obey them is like a foolish man who builds his house on loose sand.（任何一個聽到我的教誨，但不遵照著做的人就像一個愚蠢的人，他將房子建在鬆散的沙土上。）

→ 上兩句中的兩個 who 都是關係代名詞。

◇ Those who foolishly sought power by riding the back of the tiger ended up inside.（那些傻傻的騎在虎背上追尋權力的人最後進了老虎肚。）

→ 這句中的 who 也是關係代名詞。

現在讓我們來看看有關 **Who** 的謎題：

1 **Q**: Who are the best book keepers?（誰是最好的藏書人？）

A: The people who never return the books you lend them.（那些向你借書從不歸還的人。）

2 **Q**: Who always has a number of movements on foot for making money?

（誰常用腳做很多動作來賺錢？）

A: Dancing teacher.（教舞的老師。）

3 **Q**: Who sees farther than a giant does?

（誰比巨人看得更遠？）

A: Anyone who stands on his shoulder.

（任何一個站在他肩上的人。）

4 **Q**: Who is the most painstaking professional man?

（誰是最用心專業的人？）

A: The dentist.（牙醫。）

· **painstaking** [ˋpenzˌtekɪŋ] *adj.* 用心的，精心的

Anyone who stands on a giant's shoulder sees farther.

5 **Q** : Who are the best acrobats in your house?（你家中最好的特技師是誰？）

A : The pitchers and the tumblers.（水壺〔投手〕和玻璃杯〔翻筋斗的人〕。）

· pitcher [ˋpɪtʃɚ] *n.* 投手；用來喝啤酒的長杯子

> 有句諺語：“Little pitchers have long ears.”
>
> （字譯：小壺有長耳。意譯：兒童耳聰。）

6 **Q** : Who is a man who always finds a thing dull?

（誰總覺得事情乏味／誰總發現東西是鈍的？）

A : A scissors grinder.（磨剪刀的人。）

→ 磨剪刀的人每天磨鈍的 (dull) 剪刀，當然會覺得事情乏味囉。

· dull [dʌl] *adj.* 乏味的；鈍的

· thing [θɪŋ] *n.* 事情；東西

2 *When*

6W1H 的第二個字是 When。When 可作疑問詞或關係代名詞。

我們先舉若干例子：

◇ When were you born?（你何時出生？）→ 這句的 when 是疑問詞。

◇ Do you know the time when he came here?（你知道他來這裡的時間嗎？）

→ 這句中的 when 是代名詞。

◇ When the trees bow down their heads, the wind is passing by.

（當樹低下它們的頭的時候，風正從旁通過。）

◇ When the leaves hang trembling, the wind is passing through.

（當樹葉懸掛著抖動時，風正從中吹過。）

有關 When 的謎題很多。例如：

When does a mother say when?（什麼時候一位媽媽說「何時？」）

→ 這樣翻譯是不對的。"Say when." 是媽媽抱小孩上廁所時問：「好了沒？」的問語。

現在讓我們來看看有關 When 的謎題：

1 Q：When is a door not a door?（什麼時候門不是門？）

A：When it is a jar (ajar).（當它是一個甕〔半開〕的時候。）

→ a jar 與 ajar 同音。

‧ ajar [ə`dʒɑr] *adj.* 半開的

2 Q：When is a doctor like an angry man?（醫生什麼時候像一個生氣的人？）

A：When he loses his patience (patients).（當他發脾氣〔失去病人〕時。）

→ patients 與 patience 音相近。

3 Q：When is a trunk emotional?（箱子何時是易動情的？）

A：When it is empty and easily moved.（當它是空的且易於移動時。）

→ empty 可作「空虛」解。moved 是 move 的過去分詞，亦可作「受感動」解釋。

例 He is easily moved.（他容易受到感動。）

　　He is greatly moved.（他深受感動。）

4 Q : When is an artist unhappy?（藝術家什麼時候不高興？）

　A : When he draws a long face.（當他畫一張長臉時。）

→ 人在生氣時臉會拉長。高興時臉的肌肉向左右拉，所以臉會呈圓形。若說：to draw a long face 表示不高興，則 to draw a round face 應該表示高興才對。to draw a long face 字譯：畫一張長臉；意譯：拉下長臉，不高興。

When a artist draws a long face, he is unhappy.

5 Q : When is a department store like a boat?（何時百貨公司像一艘船？）

　A : When it has sales (sails).（當它有拍賣〔帆〕時。）

→ sails 與 sales 同音。

6 Q : When is a roast beef highest in price?（何時烤牛肉最貴？）

　A : When it is rarest.（當它最稀有／烤得最生的時候。）

→ beef 的三種烤法：rare (生的)，medium (半生半熟) 和 well done (很熟)。

・**rare** [rɛr] *adj.* 生的

・**rarest** [rɛrst] *adj.* 最生的

⑦ Q：When is a man like a pony?（一個人何時像一匹小馬？）

A：When he is a little hoarse (horse).（當他有點沙啞時。）

→ a little horse 與 a little hoarse 同音。

· hoarse [hors] *adj.* 聲音沙啞

⑧ Q：When is a ship at sea not on water?

（何時海上的船不在水上？）

A：When it is on fire.

（當它著火時／在火上。）

· on fire 失火，著火

When a ship at sea is on fire, it is not on water.

⑨ Q：When is a window like a star?（何時窗戶像星星？）

A：When it is a skylight.（當它是天光時。）

→ skylight 亦作「天窗」解。

⑩ Q：When are two apples alike?（何時兩個蘋果相似？）

A：When they are paired (pared).（當它們是一對時〔被削皮時〕。）

→ The apples are pared.（蘋果被削皮。）

⑪ Q：When is a baby like a china cup?（嬰兒何時像瓷杯？）

A：When it's teething (tea thing).（當它在長牙時〔茶具〕。）

→ teething (正在長牙) 與 tea thing (茶具) 同音。

⑫ Q：When is a boy not a boy?（何時男孩不是男孩？）

A：When he's a bed (abed).（當他是一張床〔睡在床上〕時。）

→ 請參看第(11)題。

⑬ Q：When is a man both hospitable and a cheat at the same time?

（一個人何時既慇懃而同時又是騙徒？）

A：When he takes you in.（當他接納你時。）

→ take in 亦作「欺騙」解。

例 He takes her in. （他欺騙她。）

14 Q : When is a chicken a glutton?（雞何時是貪吃的人？）

A : When he takes a peck at a time.（當它一次吃一配克時。）

→ 一配克約二加侖之容量。

・peck [pɛk] *n.* 配克；*v.* 啄

例 He takes a peck at a time.（他一次啄食一口。）

15 Q : When is a clock on the stairs dangerous?（臺階上的鐘何時危險？）

A : When it runs down and strikes one.

　　　（當它滾下來並且打到一個人的時候／當它慢慢停下來敲打一點時。）

→ 機械鐘錶因未上發條而停下來，可用 run down 來表示；機器因缺乏能源供應而
　　停下來也可用 run down 二字。

例 The clock strikes three.（鐘敲打三下）→表示三點

棒球主審喊：“Strike!”代表「好球」。

16 Q : When is coffee like the surface of the earth?（咖啡何時像地球表面？）

A : When it is ground.（當它被磨時／當它是地時。）

・ground [graʊnd] *v.* **(grind/ ground/ ground)** 磨 *n.* 地

另有一些動詞的三態變化跟 grind 相似，例：

find/ found/ found　發現

bind/ bound/ bound　綑綁

wind/ wound/ wound　纏繞

17 Q : When are eyes not eyes?（何時眼睛不是眼睛？）

A : When the wind makes them water.

　　　（當風吹得他們流淚時／當風把他們變成水時。）

→ water 當動詞用時，可作「流口水」解。例：My mouth waters. (我流口水。)
　　但流鼻水就要說成：My nose runs. (我流鼻水)。切不可譯成「我的鼻子在跑」！

⑱ Q：When is an apple not an apple?（何時蘋果不是蘋果？）

A：When it's a crab.（當它是野蘋果時。）

→ crab 亦作「蟹」解。德文的「癌症」就是 "Krab"，即英文的 crab。因螃蟹橫行，猶如癌四處蔓延一樣。

⑲ Q：When is music like vegetables?（何時音樂像蔬菜？）

A：When there are two beats (beets) to a measure.

　　（當一個音節裡有兩個節拍〔甜菜〕時。）

→ 另一解是「當有兩根甜菜去秤量時。」

⑳ Q：When is a nose not a nose?（何時鼻子不是鼻子？）

A：When it is a little radish (reddish).（當它是小蘿蔔時〔有點紅時〕。）

→ radish 與 reddish 讀音相近。

㉑ Q：When is a plant like a pig?（何時植物像隻豬？）

A：When it begins to root.（當它開始掘土／生根時。）

‧ root [rut] *v.* 生根；豬等動物以鼻掘土；數學中的根號

‧ square root 平方根

例 The square root of 4 is 2.（$\sqrt{4}=2$。）

㉒ Q：When is a rope like a boy at school?（繩子何時像學校裡的孩子？）

A：When it is taut (taught).（當它拉緊〔受教育〕時。）

→ taut 與 taught 音同。

例 He is taught.（他被教。）

‧ taught [tɔt] *v.* (teach/ taught/ taught) 教導

㉓ Q：When is a piece of wood like a queen?（何時一片木頭像皇后？）

A：When it is made a ruler.（當它做成一把尺／做統治者的時候。）

‧ ruler [`rulɚ] *n.* 尺；統治者

㉔ Q：When is a sailor not a sailor?（何時水手不是水手？）

A：When he's a board (aboard).（當他是一塊木板〔在船上〕時。）

→ a board (一塊木板) aboard [ə`bord] (在船上) 二者同音。

25 **Q**：When is a ship in love?（船何時在談戀愛？）

A：When she seeks a mate.（當她尋求一位配偶／大副時。）

26 **Q**：When a shoemaker is ready to make a shoe, what is the first thing he looks for?（當鞋匠準備做鞋時，最先尋找什麼東西？）

A：The last.（最後一樣東西／鞋模。）

27 **Q**：When is a shoemaker like a doctor?（何時鞋匠像醫生？）

A：When he is heeling (healing).（當他在裝鞋後跟〔在治病〕時。）

→ heeling 與 healing 同音。

28 **Q**：When is a man greatly tickled but doesn't laugh?

（人何時被大呵癢而不笑？）

A：When a fly lands on his nose.（當一隻蒼蠅歇在他的鼻子上時。）

29 **Q**：When is a trunk like two letters of the alphabet?

（旅行箱何時像字母組中的兩個字母？）

A：When it is empty (MT).（當它是空〔MT〕的時候。）

→ 將 empty 講快一點時，與 MT 二字的讀音相近。

30 **Q**：When are potatoes used for mending clothes?

（馬鈴薯何時用來補衣服？）

A：When they are put in patches.（當它們被放進田圃時／用作補釘時。）

31 **Q**：When is a loaded wagon like a forest?

（一輛滿載的運貨馬車何時像一座森林？）

A：When it is full of trunks.（當它裝滿了箱子／樹幹時。）

32 **Q**：When is a wall like a fish?（牆何時像魚？）

A：When it is scaled.（當它被攀登／剝鱗時。）

→ 徒手爬牆可用 to scale a wall，空手爬山也可說成 to scale a mountain。

33 **Q**：When is a river like the letter T?（河流何時像字母 T？）

A : When it must be crossed.（當它必須被渡過／加一橫時。）

→ 有人寫 t 忘了加一橫，寫 i 忘了打一點，所以老師教學生時注意 "Don't forget to cross your t and dot your i."。

34 Q : When is the wind like a wood chopper?（何時風像個伐木工人？）

A : When it is cutting.（當它在砍伐時。）

→ The wind is cutting. 可解釋為「風吹得很冷，刺肌割膚」。

35 Q : When is an altered dress like a secret?

（一件修改過的衣服何時像一個祕密？）

A : When it is let out.（當它被放寬／秘密被洩漏出去時。）

· **let out** 放大；洩露

例 My coat must be let out.（我的外套必須放大。）

· **to take in** 縮小

例 My coat must be taken in.（我的外套必須改小一點。）

36 Q : When is a house like a crow?（房子何時像烏鴉？）

A : When it has wings.（當它有翼／廂房時。）

37 Q : When is the time on a clock like the whistle on a train?

（鐘上的時間何時像火車上的汽笛？）

A : When it's two to two (toot toot toot).

（當它與兩點差兩分的時候〔汽笛嘟嘟嘟時〕。）

→ two to two 與 toot toot toot 音相近。

· **toot** [tut] *n.* 嘟（汽笛的鳴聲）

有一段有關 **toot** 一字的趣文是這樣寫的：

Bean, bean, the magic fruit. The more you eat, the more you toot.

（豆子，豆子，神奇的食物。你吃得越多，你就越會嘟〔放屁聲〕。）

38 Q : When is a piece of string like a stick of wood?

（一根線何時像一根木棍？）

A：When it has knots in it.（當上面有結的時候。）

→ 木頭上的節，樹上的節，線上的結都稱為 knot。

㊴ Q：When does a boat show affection?（船何時示愛？）

A：When it hugs the shore.（當它緊抱／靠近海岸時。）

· hug [hʌg] *v.* 緊抱

· embrace [ɪm`bres] *v.* 擁抱

㊵ Q：When does a chair dislike you?（椅子何時討厭你？）

A：When it is broken and can't bear you.

　　（當它壞了而無法支持你／當它痛心而無法忍受你的時候。）

· broken [`brokən] *v.* (break/ broke/ broken) 打破

例 The plate is broken.（盤子破了。）

　My heart is broken.（我心已碎。）

　I have a broken heart.（我有一顆破碎的心。）

· bear [bɛr] *v.* (bear/ bore/ born) 生育；忍受

例 The tree bears figs every year.（這棵樹每年長無花果。）

　I can't bear it.（我無法忍受。）

㊶ Q：When does a leopard change
　　　its spots?

　　　（豹何時改變斑點／位置？）

A：When he moves.

　　（當牠移動時。）

→ spot 亦作「地點」解。

When a leopard moves, it changes its spot.

㊷ Q：When does a man never fail to keep his word?

　　　（一個人何時絕對會信守諾言？）

A：When no one will take it.（當無人相信／收取他的話的時候。）

· fail to 不會

例 To keep one's word. （遵守約言。）

　　He never keeps his word. （他從未遵守約言。）

→ 不能說 to keep one's words。word 在此不能加 s。

· take it 拿去

例 You can keep it. （你可保有它。）

→ 表示你可擁有它，意思是 "I'll give it to you."。

㊸ Q : When the clock strikes thirteen, what time is it?

　　（當鐘敲了十三下時，那是什麼時刻？）

A : Time to have the clock fixed. （該修理鐘的時候。）

→ 正常的鐘頂多只敲十二下，敲十三下當然是出了問題。俗語罵人十三點，就表
　　示這人不正常，出了問題。

---

heve 在此為使役動詞，意為要某人做某事的意思。

{ I fix the clock. （我修鐘。）
{ I have the clock fixed. （我拿鐘給人修。）

{ I cut my hair. （我剪我的頭髮。）
{ I have my hair cut. （我叫人剪我的頭髮。）

to have 後面受詞的補語是過去分詞，但若 to have 後面的受詞不是物而是人，則補語
要用原形動詞。例：

I have him cut my hair. （我叫他剪我的頭髮。）

I have him fix my clock. （我叫他修我的鐘。）

㊹ Q : When does a brave heart turn to stone?（一顆勇敢的心何時變成石頭？）

A : When it becomes a little bolder (boulder).

　　（當它變的更勇敢〔一塊圓石〕時。）

→ bolder 與 boulder 同音。

· bold [bold] *adj.* 勇敢；bolder 更勇敢

· boulder [`boldɚ] *n.* 圓石

提到 bold 這個字，就會聯想起一則有趣的笑話。曾演過「國王與我」(*The King and I*) 的名演員光頭影帝尤伯連納在應徵演員時問導演 "How can I be a famous actor?" （我如何能成為名演員？）導演回答："You must be bold!"（你必須勇敢！）於是他回去把頭剃得光光的，成了禿頭。次日去見導演說："Now I am bald." 原來他將 bold [bold] 聽成了 bald [bɔld]（禿的）。

45 Q：When is a man where he never is and never could be?

（一個人何時在他從沒到過且絕不可能到過的地方？）

A：When he is beside himself.（當他在他自己旁邊時。）

· **be beside oneself** 神經錯亂，發怒

例 He is beside himself with anger.（他發怒而失去自主。）

46 Q：When a boy falls into the water, what is the first thing he does?

（當小孩掉進水裡時，他做的第一件事是什麼？）

A：Gets wet.（弄濕了。）

47 Q：When do broken bones begin to make themselves useful?

（斷骨何時使它們自己變得有用？）

A：When they begin to knit.（當它們開始編織／長合時。）

48 Q：When does a candle get angry?（蠟燭何時生氣？）

A：When it is put out or when it flares up.（當它被吹滅或忽燃的時候。）

→ be put out 亦可作「憂傷」解。flare up 亦作「震怒」解。

49 Q：When can your coat pocket be empty and yet have something in it?（你的外套口袋何時空空如也，卻仍有東西在裡面？）

A：When it has a hole in it.（當裡面有個洞的時候。）

→ 裡面什麼都沒有，至少還有個洞。

50 Q：When a man complains that his coffee is cold, what does his wife do?（當一個人抱怨咖啡是冷的時候，他的太太做什麼？）

A：She makes it hot for him.（她使他難受／她為他把它加熱。）

· to make it hot for one = to make one's life unpleasant

　使某人難受，日子不好過

(51) Q : When a man faints, what

　　　number will restore him?

　　　（當一個人昏倒時，什麼數目

　　　能使他甦醒過來？）

　A : You must bring him 2.

　　　（你必須給他2。）

→ to 與 two 音相近。

· to bring one to　使某人甦醒

· to bring him to　使他甦醒

When a man faints, you must bring him to (two).

(52) Q : When does a farmer perform miracles?（農夫何時表演奇蹟？）

　A : When he turns his horse to grass and turns his cows to pasture.

　　　（當他把馬變成草／趕到草地，而把牛變成草原／牽到牧場的時候。）

(53) Q : When are oysters like fretful people?（牡蠣何時像易生煩惱的人？）

　A : When they're in a stew.（當它們在燉／焦慮的時候。）

· in a stew　憤怒

例 He is in a stew.（他憤怒。）

(54) Q : When can you be said to

　　　have four hands?

　　　（何時你可以說有四隻手？）

　A : When you double your

　　　fists.（當你握拳時。）

→ double 亦作「加倍」解。

· double your fists　握拳

You double your fist.

W 的發音就是 "double U"，把 U 加倍就成了 W。

55 **Q** : When does a ship tell a falsehood?（船何時説謊？）

A : When she lies at the wharf.（當她靠在碼頭／對碼頭説謊時。）

→ lie 亦作「説謊」解。

· to lie at 靠在

注意 lie 的三態變化：

lie/ lay/ lain 躺，臥

lie/ lied/ lied 説謊

---

56 **Q** : When can you say that a public speaker is a thief of lumber?

（你何時能説一個演説家是竊木賊？）

A : When he takes the floor.（當他拿走地板／演説時。）

· to take the floor 演説，發言

· take the floor （在會議中）請某人發言

57 **Q** : When is a sick man a contradiction?（一個病人何時是一種矛盾？）

A : When he is an impatient patient.（當他是一個不耐煩的病人時。）

· patient [`peʃənt] *n.* 病人；*adj.* 耐煩的

58 **Q** : When do your teeth take over the functions of your tongue?

（你的牙齒何時取代你的舌頭的功能？）

A : When they start to chatter.（當他們開始喋喋不休／顫抖做響時。）

· chatter [`tʃætɚ] *v.* 喋喋不休，震顫作響

例 She is chattering at me.（她對我喋喋不休的説。）

My teeth are chattering with cold.（我的牙齒因寒冷而震顫作響。）

59 **Q** : When does an automobile go exactly as fast as a train?

（汽車何時跟火車跑得一樣快？）

A : When it is on the train.（當它在火車上時。）

60 **Q** : When may we say a student is very hungry?

（我們何時可以説一個學生很餓？）

A : When he devours his books. （當他吞食／如飢似渴地讀書本時。）

⑥⑴ Q : When does a bather capture a large bird?

（沐浴者何時會捉到一隻大鳥？）

A : When he takes a duck in the water.

（當他在水中捉到一隻鴨／將頭浸入水中時。）

⑥⑵ Q : When should any pig be able to write?（何時豬都應該會寫字？）

A : When he has been turned into a pen.

（當牠已經變成一支鋼筆／被關進圍欄時。）

⑥⑶ Q : When is a bill like an old chair that is repaired?

（帳單何時像一張舊的而且已修好的椅子？）

A : When it is receipted (reseated).（當它被蓋「已付款」印〔更換坐墊〕時。）

→ reseated 更換坐墊，即 put a new seat on。receipted 與 reseated 同音。

· **receipt** [rɪ`sit] *n.* 收據；*v.* 收到

③ *Where*

　　6W1H 的第三個字是 Where。Where 可用作疑問詞，也可用作關係代名詞。例如：

◇ Who has seen the wind?（誰見過風？）

◇ This is the place where he was born.（這是他出生的地方。）

◇ Where am I?（這是什麼地方？）切不可譯成「我在哪裡。」

　　現在讓我們來看看有關 Where 的謎題：

1 Q : Where are you likely to go when you are fourteen years old?

　　　　（當你十四歲時你會到哪裡去？）

A : Into your fifteenth.（向你的十五歲邁進。）

2 Q : Where are the kings of England usually crowned?

　　　　（英王通常在何處加冕？）

A : On the head.（在頭上。）

→ 皇冠當然要加到頭上。

3 Q : Where can everyone always find money when he looks for it?

　　　　（當每個人尋找錢的時候，何處總可以找得到？）

A : In the dictionary.（在字典裡。）

→ 字典裡一定有 money (錢) 這個字。

4 Q : Where will you find the center of gravity?

　　　　（你在哪裡可以找到重心的中心？）

A : At the letter V.（字母 V。）

→ gravity 這字的中心就是 V。

5 Q : Where is the best place to be fat?（何處是發胖最好的地方？）

A : At the butcher shop.（在肉店裡。）

→ 題中的 to be fat 的 to be 可作「成為」解，而 fat 一字亦作「脂肪」解。

6 Q: Where do you have the longest view in the world?

（你在世界上何處有最長的視野？）

A: By a roadside where there are telephone poles, because there you can see from pole to pole.（在有電桿的路邊，因為在那裡，你能從一根電桿〔一極〕看到另一根電桿〔另一極〕。）

→ 此題 pole 作「桿」或「極」解。例如：south pole 南極；north pole 北極。

7 Q: Where is there fire?（何處有火？）

A: Where there is smoke, there is fire.（有煙之處就有火。）

→ 這是一句有名的諺語，意思是「無風不起浪」，「事出必有因」。

Where there is smoke, there is fire.

4 *What*

6W1H 的第四個字是 What。What 可用作疑問詞或帶動子句之用。例如：

◊ What is your father?（你父親從事何種職業？）

◊ What is yours is mine.（你所有的東西都是我的。）

◊ What is mine is yours.（我所有的東西都是你的。）

◊ I understand what you say.（我了解你所說的。）

◊ Force is what makes an object accelerate.

（力者物之所由而奮者也／力是使一個物體加速的東西。）

→ 此即牛頓第二運動定律，其公式 f = ma，f 為力 (force)，m 為質量 (mass)，a 為加速度 (acceleration)。

現在讓我們來看看有關 What 的謎題：

1 Q: What is the worst weather for rats and mice?

（什麼是對老鼠最糟的天氣？）

A: When it rains cats and dogs.（下貓下狗／傾盆大雨。）

→ 這句通俗的成語典故聽說是這樣的：有一年英國倫敦大雨，很多貓狗都被沖到泰晤士河中，有人以為是天上下的貓和狗，於是形成這句 "It rains cats and dogs."。

2 Q: What is worse than finding a worm in an apple?

（什麼比在蘋果裡發現一條蟲更糟？）

A: Finding half a worm.

（發現半條蟲。）

Finding half a worm is worse than finding a worm.

→ 當發現半條蟲時，另一半可能已下肚了。

3 Q： What word is usually pronounced wrong, even by the best of scholars?（什麼字經常會被唸錯，即使是最好的學者亦然？）

A： Wrong, of course.（當然是「錯」。）

4 Q： What question is it to which you positively must answer "Yes"?

（什麼問題你肯定必須回答「是」？）

A： How does Y-E-S pronounce?（Y-E-S 如何發音？）

5 Q： What is the most contradictory sign seen in a library?

（在圖書館裡看到的那一個標語最矛盾？）

A： To speak aloud is not allowed (aloud).

（大聲說話是不被允許的〔大聲的〕。）

→ allowed 與 aloud 同音，乍聽之下變成 To speak aloud is not aloud.（大聲說話不算大聲。）豈不矛盾？

6 Q： What question can never be answered by "Yes?"

（什麼問題絕不能用「是」來回答？）

A： Are you asleep?（你睡著了嗎？）

當然也可以問 "Are you dead?"（你死了嗎？）這種問題當然不能答 "Yes!"

7 Q： What salad is best for newlyweds?（什麼生菜對新婚夫婦最好？）

A： Lettuce alone.（只要萵苣。）

→ 新婚燕爾，卿卿我我，只要 Lettuce 就好。"Lettuce alone." 與 "Let usalone." 同音。例：Let us alone.（讓我們獨處。）

8 Q： What relation is the doorstep to the doormat?（門階到門墊是何關係？）

A： A step-father (farther).（繼父〔一步之遙〕。）

→ farther 與 father 讀音相近。farther 是 far 的比較級。

9 Q： What is the most disagreeable month for soldiers?

（最不適士兵的月份是什麼？）

A : A long March. （漫長的三月。）

→ march 亦作「行軍」解。"A long march." 為長途行軍。

⑩ Q : What is the only thing you can break when you say its name?

（什麼東西當你一説出它的名字就把它給打破了？）

A : Silence. （寧靜。）

→ 當你說「寧靜」這個詞的時候，你已打破「寧靜」了。

⑪ Q : What is the oldest piece of furniture in the world?

（世界上最古老的傢俱是什麼？）

A : The multiplication table. （九九乘法表。）

· table [`tebl] *n.* 桌子，表

· time table 時刻表

⑫ Q : What walks over the water and under the water, yet does not touch the water? （什麼在水的上方行走又在水的下方行走，卻不碰到水？）

A : A woman crossing a bridge over a river with a pail of water on her head. （一位婦女頭上頂著一桶水走過一座跨河的橋。）

→ 婦女在河水之上，又在桶裡的水之下，當然碰不到水。

⑬ Q : What is the coldest place in a theater? （電影院裡什麼地方最冷？）

A : Z row (zero). （Z 排〔零度〕。）

→ z row 與 zero 同音。橫向為 row，稱為列；縱向為 column，稱為行。

⑭ Q : What fishes have eyes nearest together? （什麼魚的眼睛靠得最近？）

A : The smallest fish. （最小的魚。）

⑮ Q : What does a person usually grow in a garden if he works hard?

（如果一個人在花園裡努力工作，通常是種什麼？）

A : Tired. （疲勞。）

→ grow 也作「變成」解。

例 He grew old. （他變老了。）

He grows tired. （他疲倦了。）

· grow [gro] *v.* (grow/ grew/ grown) 種植；變為

16 Q : What happens to a cat when it crosses a desert on Christmas Day?（當一隻貓在聖誕節跨過沙漠時會發生什麼事？）

A : It gets sandy claws (Santa Claus).（牠的爪子會黏著沙〔聖誕老人〕。）

→ sandy claws 與 Santa Claus 讀音相近。

· sand [sænd] *n.* 沙

· sandy [sændɪ] *adj.* 沙的

17 Q : What did the big firecracker say to the little firecracker?
（大爆竹對小爆竹說些什麼？）

A : "My pop's bigger than your pop."（「我的砰砰聲比你的砰砰聲大。」）

→ 乍聽之下像是 "My papa is bigger than your papa."（「我爸爸比你爸爸大。」）

18 Q : What is the end of everything?（每件事的結尾是什麼？）

A : The letter G.（字母 G。）

→ 因 everything 的字尾是 g。

19 Q : What driver never gets arrested?（什麼司機從未被逮捕過？）

A : A screwdriver.（螺絲起子。）

> 這類謎題有點像中文的謎語：什麼馬不能騎？巴拿馬或羅馬。什麼牙不能裝？葡萄牙或西班牙。

20 Q : What room can no one enter?（什麼房間無人能進入？）

A : A mushroom.（蘑菇。）

→ mushroom 並非 room，故無人能進。這與我們所說的「天做棋盤星做子，誰人能下；地做琵琶路做弦，誰人能彈？」相似。

21 Q : What is the surest way to double your money?
（把你的錢加倍最確實的方法是什麼？）

A：Fold it.（把它對摺起來。）

→ fold 也作「倍」解，例：three fold，即三倍。

㉒ **Q**：What goes through a door, but never goes in or comes out?

（什麼東西穿過門，但絕不進門或出門？）

A：A keyhole.（鑰匙孔。）

㉓ **Q**：What fish may be said to be out of place?（什麼魚可說是不得其所？）

A：A perch in a bird cage.（鱸魚／棲木在鳥籠裡。）

→ perch 亦作「棲木」解。

㉔ **Q**：What has a hand but can't scratch itself?

（什麼東西有手但不能為自己搔癢？）

A：A clock.（時鐘。）

→ 時鐘有 hour hand（時針），minute hand（分針）和 second hand（秒針），皆為 hand，但這三種 hand 都無法為鐘搔癢。

㉕ **Q**：What flies up but still is down?（什麼東西向上飛但仍然是向下？）

A：A feather.（羽毛。）

→ down 亦作「軟毛」解。

㉖ **Q**：What is the richest country in the world?

（什麼是世界上最富有的國家？）

A：Ireland, because its capital is always Dublin.

（愛爾蘭，因為它的首都〔本金〕總是都柏林〔加倍〕。）

→ Dublin 與 doubling 音相近。"It's capital is always Dublin." 與 "It's capital is always doubling." 讀音相近。

· **capital** [`kæpətl̩] *n.* 首都；資本，本金

· **Dublin** [`dʌblɪn] *n.* 都柏林（愛爾蘭首都）

㉗ **Q**：What musical instrument should we never believe?

（什麼樂器我們絕不可相信？）

A : A lyre.（七弦豎琴。）

→ lyre 與 liar (騙子) 同音。

28 **Q** : What soap is the hardest?（什麼肥皂最硬？）

A : Castile (cast steel).（橄欖香皂〔鑄鋼〕。）

→ 二者發音相近。

29 **Q** : What are the most difficult ships to conquer?（什麼船最難征服？）

A : Hardships (hard ships).（困難〔硬船〕。）

→ 二者發音相同。

30 **Q** : What is the best and cheapest light?（什麼是最好又最便宜的燈？）

A : Daylight.（日光。）

→ light 也作「光」解。

31 **Q** : What is he doing as he creates a happy sound on his entire journey to a place of monetary deposit?（在他走一段很長的路到一個貨幣的存款處沿路上他發出快樂的聲音，他做什麼？）

A : Laughing all the way to the bank.（到銀行一路上歡笑。）

· monetary [ˋmʌnəˌtɛrɪ] *adj.* 貨幣的

· deposit [dɪˋpazɪt] *n.* 儲蓄；存放

32 **Q** : What is the well-known saying obtained by changing one letter in each word? TAPE TIE PULL MY TOE CORNS

（改變上列每個單字的一個字母，可得到一句大家都知道的說法，是那一句？）

A : Take the bull by the horns.（挺身面對困難。）

→ TAPE → TAKE   TIE → THE   PULL → BULL   MY → BY

TOE → THE   CORNS → HORNS

33 **Q** : What are the same seven letters in the same order that, when filled in the blanks, make the sentence express a complete sense?

（哪七個字母以同一順序填入空格中，就可使句子表達一完整的意義？）

A ___(a)___ waiter is ___(b)___ to serve the meal for he has ___(c)___ .

(a) notable (b) not able (c) no table

A : A notable waiter is not able to do the job for he has no table.

（一位有名的侍者無法做好供餐的工作因為他沒有桌子。）

→ notable 有三種拼法：notable (著名的)，not able (不能) 和 no table (沒桌子)。

㉞ Q : What is the proverb that is opposite in meaning to the proverb "Too many cooks spoil the broth"?

（與「人多易壞事」意義相反的諺語是什麼？）

A : "Many hands make light work." (「人多好辦事。」)

㉟ Q : What is the difference between an optimist and a pessimist?

（樂觀者與悲觀者之間有何差異？）

A : An optimist sees an opportunity in every calamity.

A pessimist sees a calamity in every opportunity.

（樂觀者在災難中看到機會。悲觀者在機會中看到災難。）

㊱ Q : What is the difference between houses and homes?

（房屋與家有何差異？）

A : Houses are built of brick and stone. Homes are made of love alone. (房屋乃磚石所造。家僅由愛組成。)

⑤ *Which*

6W1H 的第五個字是 Which。它可作疑問詞或關係代名詞之用，例如：

◇ Which do you prefer, tea or coffee?（你比較喜歡何者，茶或咖啡？）

◇ There was a man who had a fig which grew in his vineyard.

（從前有一個人他有一棵無花果樹，那樹長在他的葡萄園裡。）

現在讓我們來看看有關 Which 的謎語：

① **Q**: Which can move faster, heat or cold?（熱與冷那個跑得比較快？）

A: Heat, because you can catch a cold.（熱，因為你能捉到冷／感冒。）

· catch [kætʃ] *v.* (catch/ caught/ caught) 捉

· catch a cold 感冒

例 He caught a cold last week.（他上週感冒了。）

我們只聽說某人 catch a cold，未聞有人 catch heat。

You can catch a cold.

②Q: Which is the strongest day of the week?（一星期中那一天最強？）

A: Sunday, because all the rest are weak (week) days.

（星期天，因為其餘的都是弱日。）

→ 一星期中除星期天之外其餘六天稱為 week days，week 與 weak 發音相同。

Sunday is the strongest day of the week.

③Q: Which is better, complete happiness or a slice of bread?（完美的幸福或一片麵包，何者較好？）

A: A slice of bread. Nothing is better than complete happiness, and a slice of bread is better than nothing.（一片麵包。沒有東西勝於完美的幸福，而一片麵包勝於沒有東西。）

→ 即聊勝於無，若用數學大於 (>) 的符號來說，就更清楚了：

a slice of bread > nothing

nothing > complete happiness

令 $a > b$, $b > c$, ∴ $a > c$

得到的結論是：

A slice of bread is better than complete happiness.

A slice of break is better than complete happiness.

4 Q : Which takes less time to get ready for a trip, an elephant or a rooster?（那個準備好去旅行的時間較少，象或公雞？）

A : The rooster. He takes only his comb, while the elephant has to take a whole trunk.

（公雞。牠只帶梳子／雞冠，而象卻要帶一個旅行皮箱／象鼻。）

The elephant has to take a whole trunk while the rooster takes only his comb.

5 Q : Which has more legs, a horse or no horse?

（馬和非馬哪個腿比較多？）

A : No horse. No horse has five or more legs. A horse has just four legs.

（非馬。因為沒有馬〔no horse〕有五或更多條的腿，一匹馬只有四條腿。）

6 Q : Which candles burn longer, wax candles or tallow candles?

（蜜蠟燭或牛脂蠟燭，何者燒的較長？）

A : Neither. They both burn shorter.（二者皆不是。它們二者越燒越短。）

7 Q: Which is heavier, milk or cream?（何者較重，牛奶或乳酪？）

A: Milk is, because cream rises to the surface.

（牛奶較重，因為乳酪會浮在水面上。）

8 Q: Which would you rather have, a lion eat you or a tiger?

（你寧願被獅子吃掉或被老虎？）

A: Thanks, I'd rather have the lion eat the tiger.

（多謝了，我寧願獅子吃掉老虎。）

I would rather have the lion eat the tiger.

9 Q: Which day is two days before the day after the day three days after the day before Monday?

（星期一的前一天的三天後那一天後一天的前兩天是星期幾？）

A: Tuesday.（星期二。）

→ 這謎題要往英文的句子後面算起才能得到正確的答案，要注意 before 及 after 的
關係。

6 *Why*

6W1H 的第六個字是 Why。Why 可作疑問詞或引導一個子句。例如：

◇ Why does the sun go on shining?（為何太陽繼續在照耀？）

◇ Why does the sea rush to shore?（為何海水沖向岸邊？）

◇ I know the reason why the stars glow above.

（我知道星星在天空發光的理由。）

現在讓我們來看看 Why 的謎題：

1 **Q**：Why is a good student always on the run?（為何一個好學生總是在跑？）

A：Because he is always pursuing his studies.（因為他總是在追求學問。）

2 **Q**：Why can't it rain for two days continually?（為何不能連續兩天下雨？）

A：Because there is always a night in between.

（因為在兩個白天之間總有一個夜晚。）

・day [de] *n.* 天，白天

3 **Q**：Why should fish be well educated?（為何魚教育良好？）

A：Because they are so often found in schools.

（因為牠們常在學校被發現／成群出現。）

・a school of fish　一群魚

・a flock of sheep　一群羊

Fish are so offten found in schools.

4 Q : Why do carpenters believe there is no such thing as glass?

（為何木匠不相信有玻璃這東西？）

A : Because they never saw it.（因為他們從未鋸過／看過它。）

→ saw 是 see 的過去式，也當「鋸子」解，又可作動詞「鋸」之用。有一個繞口令很有趣：

Of all the saws I ever saw, I never saw a saw saw like this saw saws.

(在我所見過的鋸子中，我從未見過一把鋸子鋸東西像這把鋸子鋸的一樣。)

· saw [sɔ] *v.* (see/ saw/ seen) 看；鋸

5 Q : Why is your sense of touch impaired when you're ill?

（當你生病時，你的觸覺為何會受到損害？）

A : Because you don't feel well.（因為你會覺得不舒服。）

→ don't feel well 字譯為觸覺不好。

6 Q : Why should a lost traveler never starve in the middle of a desert?

（為何一個迷失在沙漠中的旅客絕不會挨餓？）

A : Because of the sand which is (sandwiches) there.

（因為沙〔三明治〕就在那兒。）

→ 句中 sand which is 與 sandwiches 同音。

7 Q : Why are photographers the most progressive of men?

（為何攝影師是最有進步的人？）

A : Because they are always developing.（因為他們總是在求發展／沖照。）

→ 傳統相機要用軟片，照完後要沖片，稱為 develop，例如：

Please have this film developed. (請將這軟片沖好。)

· develop [dɪˋvɛləp] *v.* 發展

8 Q : Why is tennis such a noisy game?（為何網球是很吵的比賽？）

A : Because each player raises a racket.

（因為每個球員都舉起球拍／高聲喧嘩。）

→ to raise racket 亦作「嘈雜，吵鬧」解。

9 **Q**: Why should everyone go to sleep immediately after drinking a cup

of tea?（為何每個人喝完一杯茶之後就要立刻去睡覺？）

A: Because when the T is gone, night is nigh.

（因為 T〔tea〕走了之後〔即喝完茶之後〕夜晚就近了。）

→ 將 night 字中的 t 去掉就成了 nigh。

· **nigh** [naɪ] *adj.* 在附近的

10 **Q**: Why is a river rich?（為何河流富有？）

A: Because it always has two banks.（因為它總擁有兩間銀行／兩岸。）

· **bank** [bæŋk] *n.* 銀行；河岸

11 **Q**: Why do we all go to bed?（我們為什麼都要就寢／走到床那裡去？）

A: Because the bed won't come to us.（因為床不會走到我們這邊來。）

· **go to bed** 睡覺

12 **Q**: Why is it that every man's trousers are too short?

（為何每個人的褲子都太短？）

A: Because his legs always stick out two feet.

（因為他的雙腿總會伸出兩隻腳／突出兩呎長來。）

→ foot 亦作「呎」解。(1 呎 = 12 吋，1 吋 = 2.54 公分)

13 **Q**: Why should a doctor never be seasick?（為何醫生從不暈船？）

A: Because he is so accustomed to sea (see) sickness.

（因為他對暈船已經習慣了〔慣於替病人看病〕。）

→ sea sickness (暈船) 與 see sickness (看病) 同音。

14 **Q**: Why is a doctor the meanest man on earth?

（為何醫生是世上最卑鄙的人？）

A: Because he treats you and then makes you pay for it.

（因為他請你客／醫治你卻要你付錢。）

· treat [trit] *v.* 對待；治療；*n.* 請客

例 I'll treat you. （我要請你客。）

But you pay for it. （但你要付帳。）

(15) Q: Why are fat men sad? （為何胖子悲傷？）

A: Because they are men of sighs (size). （因為他們是悲嘆〔大塊頭〕的人。）

→ sighs 與 size 同音。

· sigh [saɪ] *n.* 嘆息

· size [saɪz] *n.* 大小

(16) Q: Why are tall people always the laziest? （為何高個子總是最懶惰的？）

A: Because they are longer in bed than short people.

（因為他們躺在床上比矮個子長／在床上的時間比矮個子長。）

(17) Q: Why does lightning shock people? （為何閃電會使人震驚？）

A: Because it doesn't know how to conduct itself.

（因為它不知道如何為人／傳導自己。）

→ to conduct oneself 即 to behave oneself，作「為人」解。

例 How did he behave himself? （他為人如何？）

He behaves himself very well. （他為人很好。）

Behave yourself! （乖一些！）

(18) Q: Why don't women become bald as soon as men?

（為何女人不會像男人那樣快變成禿頭？）

A: Because they wear their hair longer. （因為女人留的頭髮較長。）

→ 此處 longer 的含意是時間較長。

(19) Q: Why should a fisherman always be wealthy? （為何漁夫總是富有？）

A: Because all his business is net profit.

（因為他的事業是淨利／以網取利。）

· net [nɛt] *n.* 淨值；魚網

20 Q : Why is life the hardest riddle?（為何生命是最難的謎？）

A : Because everybody has to give it up.（因為每個人都得把它放棄。）

→ "Men are mortal."（凡人皆會死。），所以最後都得放棄。

21 Q : Why is it useless to send an E-mail to Washington today?

（為何今天寄電子郵件到華盛頓是無用的？）

A : Because he is dead.（因為他死了。）

→ Washington 是地名也是人名。

22 Q : Why should a spider make a good outfielder?

（為何蜘蛛可充任好的外野手？）

A : Because it is always catching flies.（因為牠會捕飛球／捕蒼蠅。）

・ fly [flaɪ] *n.* 蒼蠅 *v.* **(fly/ flew/ flown)** 飛

23 Q : Why does time fly?（時間為何會飛？）

A : Because so many people are trying to kill it.（因為很多人想要捕殺它。）

・ kill time 消磨時間

24 Q : Why did Tom's mother knit him three stockings when he was in the army?（為何湯姆在軍中時，他的母親替他編織三隻襪子？）

A : Because Tom wrote her he had gotten so tall and he had grown another foot.

（因為湯姆寫信給她，他已長得很高，又長出了一隻腳／又長高了一呎。）

25 Q : Why is the inside of everything so mysterious?

（為何每個東西的內部都很神秘？）

A : Because we can't make it out.（因為我們無法把它翻到外面來。）

・ make it out 了解，明顯表出

例 I can't make it out.（我看不出它是什麼。）

26 Q : Why should ladies who wish to remain slender avoid the letter C?

（想保持苗條身段的女士們為何要避免字母 C？）

A：Because C makes fat a fact.（因為 C 會使肥胖變成事實。）

→ fat 中間加一個 c 即成 fact 了！

> make 作為「不完全及物動詞」(incomplete transitive verb) 時，後面受詞的補語可為形容詞或原形動詞或名詞。例：
>
> He makes me angry.（他使我生氣。）→ angry 為形容詞。
> He makes me cry.（他使我哭。）→ cry 為原形動詞。
> He makes me a famous actor.（他使我成為名演員。）→ actor 為名詞。

27 Q：Why do children object to the absence of Santa Claus?

（為何小孩們都不贊成聖誕老人缺席？）

A：Because they prefer his presence (presents).

（因為他們喜歡他的出席〔禮物〕。）

→ presence (出席) 與 presents (禮物) 讀音相近。

28 Q：Why does the Statue of Liberty stand in New York Harbor?

（自由女神像為何站在紐約港？）

A：Because it can't sit down.（因為它坐不下來。）

29 Q：Why is autumn the best time for a lazy person to read a book?

（為何秋天是懶人讀書最好的時光？）

A：Because autumn turns the leaves for him.

（因為秋天能為他翻書頁／使樹葉變色。）

→ to turn the leaves 可解釋為「使樹葉變色」。

· turn over a new leaf 改過自新；重新做人

例 I have decided to turn over a new leaf and do lots of research work.

（我已決定重新開始，做大量的研究工作。）

30 Q：Why is a policeman the strongest in the world?

（為何警察是世界上最強壯的人？）

A：Because he can hold up automobiles with one hand.

（因為他能用一隻手舉起汽車。）

→ 警察一舉手，汽車即須停駛。hold up 作「停止」解。

31 Q：Why is your nose not twelve inches long?

（為何你的鼻子不是十二吋長？）

A：Because then it would be a foot.（因為這樣的話它將是一隻腳。）

→ 12 吋 = 1 呎 (foot)。

· foot [fʊt] *n.* 腳；吋

32 Q：Why is an empty purse always the same?（空錢包為何總是一樣的？）

A：Because there is never any change in it.

（因為它從未有任何改變／零錢。）

→ change 亦可作「零錢」解。

33 Q：Why does a cat look first to one side and then to the other when it enters a room?（為何貓進到房間時，先看一邊然後再看另一邊？）

A：Because it can't see both sides at once.（因為牠不能同時看兩邊）。

34 Q：Why should you never tell secrets in a cornfield?

（為何絕不可在玉米田裡談論機密？）

A：Because corn has ears and is bound to be shocked.

（因為玉米有耳〔穗〕而且必會感到震驚〔被捆成乾草堆〕。）

· ear [ɪr] *n.* 耳；穗

· be bound to 一定會

· bound [baund] *v.* (bind/ bound/ bound) 綑，綁

例 It is bound to rain soon.（過一會兒一定會下雨。）

35 Q：Why do you always make a mistake when you put on a shoe?

（當你穿鞋時，為何總是會犯錯？）

A：Because you put your foot in it.（因為你把腳放在它裡面。）

· put one's foot in it 說錯話，說話不得體

例 I really put my foot in it when I asked her how her husband was; he has left her for another woman.

（我真的不該多嘴去問她，她的丈夫如何，他已離開她跟另一個女人走了。）

36 **Q** : Why do white sheep eat more than black ones?

（為何白羊吃得比黑羊多？）

A : Because there are more of them in the world.

（因為世界上白羊比較多。）

37 **Q** : Why is a ship one of the most polite things on earth?

（為何船是世界上最有禮貌的東西？）

A : Because it always advances with a bow.

（因為它總是一面前進一面鞠躬／以船首前進。）

· bow [bo] *n.* 弓；船首

· bow [bau] *v.* 彎下，鞠躬

38 **Q** : Why does a man who has just shaved look like a wild animal?

（為何一個剛刮完鬍子的男人看來像一頭野獸？）

A : Because he has a bare face.（因為他有一張光光的臉。）

→ bare face 與 bear face 同音，乍聽之下，以為是熊臉。

A man who has just shaved has a bare face.   *a bear face*

39 Q : Why is it vulgar to sing and play by yourself?

（為何你獨自演唱是粗俗的？）

A : Because such a performance is so low (solo).

（因這種表演是低級〔獨唱〕的。）

→ solo 獨唱，與 so low 同音。

· solo [`solo] *n.* 獨唱

40 Q : Why is your nose in the middle of your face?

（為何你的鼻子長在臉的中央？）

A : Because it is a scenter (center).（因它是嗅覺〔中央〕器官。）

→ scenter 與 center 同音。

41 Q : Why are weary people like automobile wheels?

（為何疲倦的人像汽車的車輪？）

A : Because they are tired.（因為它們裝了車胎／疲倦。）

42 Q : Why should taxicab drivers be brave men?（為何計程車司機是勇者？）

A : Because "None but the brave deserve the fair (fare)."

（因為「唯勇者能得美人〔車資〕。」）

→ 上句聽起來像是 "None but the brave deserve the fare."（「唯勇者能得車資。」）

· fair [fɛr] *n.* 美人；仙女

· fare [fɛr] *n.* 車資

43 Q : Why does a coat get bigger when you take it out of a suitcase?

（當你把外套從皮箱拿出時，它為何會變大？）

A : Because you will find it increases (in creases).

（因為你會發現它增大了〔有摺痕〕。）

→ 將 increases (增加) 拆開成二字 in creases (有摺痕)，讀音相同。

· crease [kris] *n.* 皺紋，摺痕

44 Q : Why are fishermen such wonderful correspondents?

（為何漁夫是非常好的通信者？）

A : Because they always like to drop a line.

（因為他們總喜歡放根魚線／寫一兩行信。）

45 Q : Why is it impossible for a person who lisps to believe in the existence of young ladies?

（為何不可能使一個口齒不清的人相信有年輕小姐的存在？）

A : Because with him every miss is a myth.

（因為對他而言，每位小姐都是一個虛構的神話。）

→ 因為口齒不清的人會把 miss 唸成 myth。

· myth [mɪθ] *n.* 神話故事

46 Q : Why is it that when you are looking for something you always find it in the last place you look?

（為何當你尋找東西時，你總在最後尋找的地方找到？）

A : Because you always stop looking when you find it.

（因為當你找到時，你就不找了。）

47 Q : Why is paper money more valuable than coins?

（為何紙幣比硬幣更有價值？）

A : When you put it in your pocket, you double it, and when you take it out, you find it still in creases.（當你把紙幣放進口袋時，其價值加倍／對摺起來，而當你把它取出時，你發現它仍在增值／有摺痕。）

→ in creases (有摺痕) 與 increases (增加) 同音。請參看第(43)題。

48 Q : Why does a bald-headed man have no use for keys?

（為何鑰匙對秃頭漢毫無用處？）

A : Because he has lost his locks.（因為他已丟掉了他的鎖／頭髮。）

→ locks 可作「頭髮」解。

· lock [lɑk] *n.* 鎖

49 **Q** : Why should you never swim in the River Seine at Paris?

（為何你絕不可在巴黎的塞茵河游泳？）

A : Because if you did, you would be insane (in Seine).

（因為若然，你就會發瘋〔在塞茵河裡〕。）

→ insane 與 in Seine 同音。

50 **Q** : Why should you expect a fire in a circus to be very destructive?

（為何你認為馬戲團裡的火很有破壞性？）

A : Because it is intense (in tents).（因為它很強烈〔在帳篷裡〕。）

→ intense 與 in tents 同音。

51 **Q** : Why should a dishonest man always stay indoors?

（為何不誠實的人總留在室內？）

A : So no one will ever find him out.

（所以沒人會發現他外出／沒人能發覺他。）

→ find out 作「發現」解。

例 He often cheated me, but at last I found him out.

（他常騙我，但終被我發現了。）

52 **Q** : Why can hens lay eggs only during the day?

（為何母雞只在白天下蛋？）

A : Because at night they become roosters.

（因為到晚上牠們都變成了公雞。）

→ roost 作「休息處」解。rooster 亦可作「休息者」解。晚上母雞歇息，自然就成了「休息者」。

53 **Q** : Why are passengers in airplanes so polite to each other?

（為何飛機上的乘客彼此彬彬有禮？）

A : For fear of falling out.（唯恐掉出來／起爭吵。）

→ fall out 作「爭吵」解。例如：

They have fallen out with each other over the education of their children.
（他們為孩子的教育問題互相爭吵不休。）

54 **Q** : Why is an empty matchbox superior to all others?

（為何一個空火柴盒比其他的都優越？）

A : Because it is matchless.（因為它沒有火柴／無可匹敵。）

→ match 可作「匹敵」或「對手」解，亦作「火柴」解。

55 **Q** : Why does the tight rope dancer always have to repeat his performance?（為何走鋼索的人總得重複其表演？）

A : Because he is always on cord (encore).

（因為他總是在繩索上〔再來一個〕。）

→ on cord (在繩索上) 與 encore (再來一個) 音相近。

・cord [kɔrd] *n.* 繩索

・encore [`aŋkor] *n.*（法文）再來一個，再演一次

56 **Q** : Why does a warm day give an icicle a bad reputation?

（為何暖和的天氣給冰柱壞的聲譽？）

A : Because it turns it into an eavesdropper.

（因為它使冰柱成為偷聽者／屋簷水滴。）

・icicle [`aɪ,sɪkl̩] *n.* 冰柱

・eaves [`ivz] *n.* 屋簷

・eavesdrop [`ivz,drɑp] *v.* 偷聽

・eavesdropper [`ivz,drɑpɚ] *n.* 偷聽者

57 **Q** : Why is a gardener the most extra ordinary man in the world?

（為何園丁是世上最傑出的人？）

A : Because he has more business on earth than any other man;

（因為在世上的業務他比任何人多／對泥土他比任何人有更多的工作。）

he has good grounds for what he does;

（對他所做的事他有很好的理由／他有很好的土做他的工作。）

he is master of the mint;（他是造幣廠的廠長／薄荷樹的主人。）

he sets his own time (thyme);

（他安排他自己的時間〔他種植自己的百里香草〕。）

and better still, he can raise his own salary (celery) every year.

（更好的是，他能每年自行加薪〔每年他自己種芹菜〕。）

· mint [mɪnt] *n.* 薄荷；鑄幣廠

· thyme [taɪm] *n.* 百里香

· salary [ˋsælərɪ] *n.* 薪水

· celery [ˋsɛlərɪ] *n.* 芹菜

7 *How*

6W1H 的第七個字是 How。我們最先學會的 how 的用法是：

◊ **How are you?**（你好嗎？）

◊ **How do you do!**（幸會！）

→ 回答 "How do you do?" 就是同樣說："How do you do!"。

現在讓我們來看看有關 **How** 的謎題：

1 Q： How long is a string?（一根線有多長？）

A： Just twice as long as half its length.（剛好是它一半的兩倍長。）

> 同樣若有人問："**How heavy is a pig?**"（「一隻豬多重？」）你也可以俏皮的說：
> "**Just twice as heavy as half its weight.**"（「剛好是牠重量一半的兩倍。」）

2 Q： How can five people divide five cookies so that each gets a cookie and yet one cookie remains on the plate?

（五人分五個餅，每人分一個之後，還有一個餅留在盤子裡，如何分法？）

A： The last person takes the plate with the cookie.

（最後一個人連盤帶餅一起拿走。）

3 Q： How can you always have what you please?

（你如何才總能得到你所喜歡的東西？）

A： By always being pleased with what you have.

（你總是喜歡你所擁有的東西。）

→ 喜歡你所擁有的東西，當然你就擁有你所喜歡的東西了。

4 Q： How can you make a thin child fat?（如何把瘦小孩變胖？）

A： Throw him into the air and he'll come down plump.

（把他拋到空中，他就會噗通落下來／肥胖起來。）

· plump [plʌmp] *adj.* 胖嘟嘟

· come down plump 摔得很重

⑤ Q: How can you make a coat last?

（如何才能使外套耐穿／如何使外套成為最後？）

A: Make the trousers and vest first.（先做褲子和背心。）

⑥ Q: How do we know that a dentist is unhappy in his work?

（我們怎麼知道牙醫在工作時不快樂？）

A: Because he looks down in the mouth.

（因為他看起來很沮喪／從口裡往下看。）

· look down in the mouth

看起來沮喪、愁眉苦臉

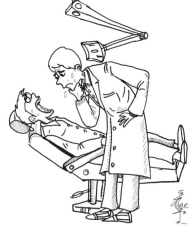

He looks down in the mouth.

⑦ Q: How do locomotives hear?

（火車頭要如何聽？）

A: Through their engineers (engine-ear).（藉由他們的工程師〔引擎耳〕。）

→ engineer 與 engine-ear 同音。engineer 一字亦可視為：

engineer = engine + near，讀音相近。

⑧ Q: How can you best learn the value of money?

（如何才能了解錢的價值？）

A: By trying to borrow some.（試著借些錢。）

⑨ Q: How would you most easily swallow a door?

（你如何輕易地把一扇門吞下去？）

A: By bolting it.（把它閂住／吞下。）

· bolt [bolt] v. 閂住；吞食

例 He bolted his food.（他急忙吞下食物。）

He bolted the door.（他閂門。）

⑩ Q : How does the fireplace feel when you fill it with coal.

（當壁爐添滿木炭時，它的感覺如何？）

A : Grateful (grate full). （感謝〔爐格滿了〕。）

→ grateful (感謝) 與 grate full 發音相近。

· grate [gret] *n.* 爐格

例 The grate is full. （爐格滿了。）

⑪ Q : How many bushel baskets full of earth can you take out of a hole that is three meters square and one meter deep?

（從一個三米見方一米深的洞可搬走多少籮筐的土？）

A : None. The earth has already been taken out.

（一筐都沒有。洞中的土早已挖走了。）

→ 既然是洞 (hole)，其中的土當然已被挖走。

⑫ Q : How would you speak of a tailor when you couldn't remember his name?（當你記不起裁縫的名字時，你如何稱呼他？）

A : As Mr. So-and-So (sew-and-sew). （稱某某先生〔縫衣先生〕。）

→ so 與 sew 同音。

⑬ Q : How can you change a pumpkin into a squash?

（如何把南瓜變成果醬？）

A : Throw it up high and it will come down a squash.

（把它拋得高高的，它就會落下摔爛／變成果醬。）

· squash [skwɑʃ] *n.* 果醬 *v.* 摔爛

⑭ Q : How is it possible to get up late in the day and yet rise when the rays of the sun first come through the window?

（如何才能在白天很晚起床，而起來時太陽光線首先照進窗戶？）

A : By sleeping in a bedroom facing the west. （睡在一間面西的臥室。）

→ 一覺睡到夕陽西下，起床時太陽正照進窗戶，還以為是朝陽初升，是黎明呢！

15 Q : How does a sailor know there is a man in the moon?

（水手怎麼知道月亮裡有一個人？）

A : Because he has been to see (sea).（因為他早就看到了〔曾經在海上〕。）

→ "He has been to sea." 與 "He has been to see." 發音同。

16 Q : How can you make a tall man short?（如何使一個高個子變矮？）

A : By borrowing a lot of money from him.（向他借很多錢。）

→ short 亦作「缺乏」解。

17 Q : How can a cat go into a cellar with four feet and come out with eight?（一隻貓如何進入地窖時有四隻腳，出來時卻有八隻腳？）

A : It catches a mouse.（牠捉到一隻老鼠。）

這裡有一個類似的謎題：

兩個爸爸和兩個兒子吃麵，一人一碗，結果只吃了三碗，是怎麼回事？

謎底：一個人跟他爸爸以及自己的兒子吃麵。

→ 祖孫三代，豈不是有兩個爸爸和兩個兒子？

⑧ *Why Are They Alike?*

① **Q**: Why are bad boy and a dirty rug alike?（為何壞孩子和髒地毯相似？）

A: Because both of them need a beating.（因為兩者都需要一頓打。）

② **Q**: Why is a coward like a leaky faucet?（為何懦夫和漏水的水龍頭相似？）

A: Because both of them run.（因為兩者都會逃／漏水。）

③ **Q**: Why are weathervanes like loafers?（為何風標像遊手好閒的人？）

A: Because they both go around doing nothing.

（因為兩者都遊盪無所事事。）

→ 風標隨風轉動，所以是 go around；遊手好閒的人四處遊走是無所事事。

例 They go around doing nothing.（他們四處遊走無所事事。）

④ **Q**: Why is a letter like a bottle of perfume?（為何一封信像一瓶香水？）

A: Because they are both sent (scent).

（因為信要被寄出，香水有 **scent**〔香氣〕。）

→ sent 與 scent 同音。scent 亦作「香水」解。

⑤ **Q**: Why are authors and chickens alike?（為何作家和雞相似？）

A: Because both of them have to scratch for a living.

（因為兩者都得要 **scratch**〔作者憑亂寫，雞憑亂抓〕才能過活。）

→ 雞為了覓食，在地上亂抓，稱為 chicken scratch。

> 編者對這個詞印象深刻，一九六八年編者赴美唸書，跟六個美國學生住一起，平時寫信回家，偶有老美在旁好奇觀看，見我信紙上七橫八豎，不知所書，便說我寫的簡直像 **chicken scratch**。

⑥ **Q**: Why are a bruise and a bubble alike?（為何瘀青和氣泡相似？）

A: Because they are both caused by a blow.

（因為兩者都是 **blow** 造成的。）

→ 前者是打，後者是吹。

7 **Q** : Why are clouds and horseback riders alike?（為何雲和騎馬的人相似？）

A : Because they both hold the rains (reins).（因為兩者都握住雨〔韁繩〕。）

・ hold [hold] *v.* (hold/ held/ held) 握；持

例 Clouds hold the rains.（雲含雨水。）

Horseback riders hold the reins.（騎馬的人握住韁繩。）

8 **Q** : Why is a bad joke like an unsharpened pencil?

（為何一則差的笑話像一枝未削尖的鉛筆？）

A : Because it has no point.（因為它沒有意思／尖頭。）

9 **Q** : Why is a baseball umpire like a dog?（為何棒球主審像一條狗？）

A : Because he wears a muzzle, snaps at flies, and is always chasing fouls (fowls).（因為他戴口套／狗戴的口套，盯住飛球／撲捉蒼蠅，而且總是找犯規的動作〔追捕家禽〕。）

10 **Q** : Why is a hat on the head like a bucket full of water?

（為何戴在頭上的帽子像裝滿了水的桶？）

A : Because they are both filled to the brim.（因為兩者都是滿到邊緣。）

・ brim [brɪm] *n.* 帽緣

・ filled to the brim 滿的

例 The cup is filled to the brim.（這杯子滿到杯口。）

11 **Q** : Why are a river and a clock alike?（為何河流和鐘錶相似？）

A : Because neither of them runs without winding.

（因為沒有不上發條會走的鐘錶／沒有不蜿蜒的河。）

→ 注意 wind 當動詞用時的發音。

・ wind [waɪnd] *v.* (wind/ wound/ wound) 繞

例 I wind the clock.（我給鐘上發條。）

winding 作「蜿蜒」解。例如名曲 *"River Road"* 歌詞中的第一句就是：

River Road, River Road, winding to the sea.

That's the road leading home where I long to be, ...

（河流路，河流路，蜿蜒通到海。那是通到我渴望已久的家的道路，…）

請參見附錄 A

⑫ Q：Why are money and a secret alike?（為何錢和祕密相似？）

A：Because both of them are hard to keep.（因為兩者都不易保存。）

⑬ Q：Why are talkative people and male pigs alike?

（為何多話的人和公豬相像？）

A：Because after a while both of them becomes bores (boars).

（因為過了一會兒之後，他們兩者變成了討厭的東西〔公豬〕。）

→ boar 公豬，與 bore 音同。

‧ bore [bor] *n.* 厭煩的事物

例 What a bore!（何等的煩惱！）

⑭ Q：Why is a mouse like hay?（為何老鼠像乾草？）

A：Because the cat'll (cattle) eat it.（因為貓要〔牛〕吃牠。）

→ 此處 cat'll 是 cat will 之縮寫，但 cat'll 與 cattle (牛) 同音。

⑮ Q：Why is a large tree like a trip around the world?

（為何大樹像環遊世界的旅行？）

A：Because its root (route) is a long one.（因為它的根〔旅程〕很長。）

→ root 與 route 同音。

⑯ Q：Why is riding in an airplane like falling downstairs?

（為何搭飛機像摔下樓梯？）

A：Because it makes you soar (sore).（因為它使你翱翔〔摔痛〕。）

‧ soar [sor] *n.* 飛翔

例 The eagle soars high in the sky.（老鷹在高空飛翔。）

‧ sore [sor] *adj.* 痛的

例 I have a sore throat.（我的喉嚨痛。）

⑰ Q：Why are some children like flannel?（為何有些小孩像法蘭絨？）

A：Because they shrink from washing.（因為他們怕洗。）

→ 有些小孩聽到洗澡便退縮不前 (shrink)；法蘭絨洗了便會縮 (shrink)。

⑱ Q：Why is a sleepless person like a piece of worn cloth?

（為何失眠的人像一塊破布？）

A：Because he has no nap.（因為他沒有午睡／破布沒有絨毛。）

・nap [næp] n. 午睡

例 I want to take a nap.（我想睡午覺。）

⑲ Q：Why are sticks of candy like horses?（為何棒棒糖像馬？）

A：Because the more you lick them the faster they go.

（因為你越舔他們消失得越快／馬越打跑得越快。）

・lick [lɪk] v. 舔；打擊

⑳ Q：Why is a dog biting its tail like a good manager?

（為何咬尾巴的狗像一個好經理？）

A：Because he is making both ends meet.

（因為他使兩端相遇／收支平衡。）

・make both ends meet　使出入相符；收支平衡

例 He has a small income, he can't make both ends meet.

（他收入甚微，入不敷出。）

㉑ Q：Why is bread like the sun?（為何麵包像太陽？）

A：Because it isn't light before it rises.

（因為太陽未升起前，天不會亮／麵包沒發起來之前，不會軟綿綿。）

→ 形容麵包軟綿綿用 light 一字。但形容飯很鬆軟要用 fluffy 一字。

㉒ Q：Why is an empty room like a room full of married people?

（為何一間空房間像一間住滿了已婚者的房子？）

A：Because there isn't a single person in it.

（因為空房間沒有一個人／單身漢住。）

→ 住滿已婚人士的房間裡沒有一個人是單身漢。

· single [`sɪŋg!] *n.* 單身漢 *adj.* 單獨一個

例 I am single.（我單身。）

㉓ **Q**：Why is a bowl of flowers on a table like a speech made on the deck of a ship?（為何桌上的一盆花像船的甲板上的一篇演說？）

A：Because it is a decoration.（因為它是一種裝飾。）

→ decoration 與 deck oration（甲板演說）同音。上句聽起來和 "It is a deck oration." 相近。

㉔ **Q**：Why is a bad cold like a great humiliation?（為何重感冒像奇恥大辱？）

A：Because it brings the proudest man to his sneeze (knees).

（因為它能使最驕傲的人打噴嚏〔最高貴的人下跪〕。）

→ his sneeze 與 his knees 同音。

㉕ **Q**：Why is a dilapidated house like old age?

（為何一幢毀損的房子像老年時期？）

A：Because its gate (gait) is feeble and its locks are few.

（因為它的門〔步態〕易破〔柔弱〕，鎖〔頭髮〕又很少。）

㉖ **Q**：Why is a person with rheumatism like a window?

（為何患風溼症的人像窗戶？）

A：Because he is full of pains (panes).（因為他充滿了痛苦〔玻璃板〕。）

→ pain (痛苦) 與 pane (窗戶玻璃板) 同音。

提到 pain 就會想到一句名諺：No pain, no gain.（沒有痛苦就沒有收穫。）

提到 pane 就會聯想起一首歌：

Joy is Like the Rain

I saw raindrops on my window.

Joy is like the rain.

Laughter runs across my pain.

Slips away and comes again.

Joy is like the rain...

請參見附錄 B1

27 Q : Why is greediness like a bad memory?（為何貪慾像很差的記性？）

A : Because it is always forgetting (for getting).

（因為它總是忘記〔為了獲得〕。）

· greedy [`gridɪ] *adj.* 貪婪的

→ 記性差的人總是忘事 (forgetting)。forgetting 與 for getting 同音。

28 Q : Why is a loaf of bread four weeks old like a mouse running into a hole in the wall?（為何一條四星期的麵包像一隻鑽進牆洞裡的老鼠？）

A : Because you can see its tail (it's stale).

（因為你能看到它的尾巴〔不新鮮〕了。）

· tail [tel] *n.* 尾巴

· stale [stel] *adj.* 不新鮮的，陳腐的

→ its tail 和 it's stale 同音。

提到 **tail** 就會聯想到一個可唬小孩的遊戲規則：

Head I win. Tail you lose.（正面我贏。反面你輸。）

→ 錢幣的正面通常是人頭像，所以稱為 head，既然正面是 head (頭)，反面當然是尾 (tail)，頭尾相對，真是有道理！

29 Q : Why is a plum pudding like the ocean?（為何葡萄布丁像海洋？）

A : Because it is full of currants (currents).（因為它充滿了葡萄乾〔潮流〕。）

· currant [`kɝənt] *n.* 葡萄乾

· current [`kɝənt] *n.* 流，潮流

· electric current 電流

· eddy current 渦流

→ currant 與 current 同音。

30 **Q**: Why is a windy orator like a whale?（為何空談的演說家像鯨魚？）

　　A: Because he always rises to spout.

　　　（因為他總是起來滔滔不絕的講／浮出水面噴水。）

· spout [spaut] v. 噴水；滔滔不絕的講

31 **Q**: Why is a healthy boy like the Republic of China?

　　　（為何一個健康的男孩像中華民國？）

　　A: Because he has good constitution.

　　　（因為他有健康的體格／完整的憲法。）

· constitution [ˌkɑnstəˋtjuʃən] n. 體格；憲法

32 **Q**: Why are a hobo and a balloon alike?（為何無業遊民與氣球相像？）

　　A: Because both are without any visible means of support.

　　　（因為兩者都沒有任何可見的維持方法／生活。）

· hobo [ˋhəubəu] n. 無業遊民

注意此字的發音，並非 [hobo]！

33 **Q**: Why is an orange like a church belfry?（為何柑橘像鐘樓？）

　　A: Because we get a peal (peel) from it.（因為我們從那裡聽到鐘聲。）

→ 吃橘子時要剝皮，橘子皮為 orange peel，香蕉皮為 banana skin。

34 **Q**: Why is a crown prince like a cloudy day?（為何加冕的王子像多雲天？）

　　A: Because he is likely to reign (rain).（因為他即將統治國家〔下雨〕。）

→ reign (統治) 與 rain (雨) 同音。

35 **Q**: Why is the tongue like an unhappy girl?

　　　（為何舌頭像一個不開心的女孩子？）

　　A: Because they are both down in the mouth.

　　　（因為他們兩者都是憂愁的／在嘴巴的下方。）

36 **Q**: Why is a thunderstorm like a hurt lion?

（為何大雷雨像一隻受傷的獅子？）

A: One pours with rain and the other roars with pain.

（其中一個大雨如注而另一個痛苦咆哮。）

→ roar (吼) 此題乃用 p 與 r 二字互換而成，即：

pours with rain ←→ roars with pain

· pour [por] *v.* 瀉，傾注

· pouring rain 傾盆大雨

例 It never rains but it pours. （不雨則已，一雨傾盆。）

37 **Q**: Why is "I shout loudly" like icecream? （為何「我大聲喊叫」像冰淇淋？）

A: Because "I shout loudly" means "I scream" and "I scream" sounds like "icecream."

（因為「我大聲喊叫」是指「我尖叫」而「我尖叫」與「冰淇淋」發音相同。）

icecream → I scream

9 *Lots of Lettuce/Letters*

　　"Lettuce alone."（只要萵苣。）的讀音與 "Let us alone."（讓我們獨處。）的讀音幾乎是一樣的，在 What 謎題中的第 7 題就是這樣寫的。現在 Lots of lettuce 與 Lots of letters 讀音相近，這類謎題大多以字母為謎底。例如：「什麼字母像海島？」謎底是「字母 T」，因為 T 在水 (water) 的中央，因 t 居於 water 一字的中間位置。類似的謎題很多，對字彙的記憶有很大的幫助。

　　現在讓我們來看看跟字母相關的謎題：

① **Q**：What helpful thing does the letter A do for a deaf woman?

　　　（字母 A 對一個聾女人有何幫助？）

　　A：It makes her hear.（它使她聽見。）

　　→ 因 a 使 her 變為 hear。

> 有一個字的變化很有趣：he → her → hear → heart
>
> 這跟國字的變化一樣有趣：一→十→士→土→王→丑→田→由→申→車→重→動→勳

② **Q**：Why should men avoid the letter A?（為何男人們要避免字母 A？）

　　A：Because it makes men mean.（因為它使男人變得卑鄙。）

　　→ a 使 men 變為 mean。

③ **Q**：In what way are the letter A and high noon alike?

　　　（字母 A 如何與正午相像？）

　　A：Both are in the middle of day.（兩者都在一天之中。）

　　→ a 在 day 之正中，noon 的時刻也是一日之正中。

④ **Q**：Why is the letter B like fire?（字母 B 為何像火？）

　　A：Because it makes oil boil.（因為它能使油沸騰。）

　　→ b 加 oil 變為 boil。

飯是 **boiled rice**，但開水卻是 **boiling water**。現在分詞與過去分詞應注意使用。

⑤ Q：Which letters are the hardest workers?（那些字母是最努力的工作者？）

　　A：The B's (bees).（字母 **B**〔蜜蜂〕。）

→ B's 與 bees 同音。

「黑板上有三個 **B** 字。」英文應寫成 "There are three B's on the blackboard."。若寫成 three B 就錯了。那一撇 (apostrophe [əˋpɑstrəfɪ]) " ' " 很重要，不可少，而且要注意撇的方向。"There are two f's in off."（off 一字中有兩個 f。）
例如："Your 8's look like S's."（你的 8 看起來像 S。）

⑥ Q：What does the letter B do for boys as they grow up?

　　　（當孩子長大時，字母 **B** 為他們做什麼？）

　　A：As they grow older, it makes them bolder.

　　　（當他們越長越大時，**B** 使他們更勇敢。）

→ 把 b 加 older 變成 bolder (bold 的比較級)。bold (勇敢的) 與 bald (禿的) 只差一個字母。兩個字很好記，因為人越老 (old) 越勇敢，所以 bold 就是勇敢的；而禿頭一定是頭光的像個球 (ball)，所以 bald 就是禿的。有關 bald 和 bold 的笑話，讀者可在其他謎題去找。

提到「禿」這個字，就會聯想到「禿驢」，也就連帶想到一位清代的才子紀曉嵐。紀才子最愛舞文弄墨，捉弄別人。一日來到廟中，見小和尚正在掃地，乃誇其氣宇非凡，將來必成有名大和尚，囑小和尚端上筆硯，寫下二聯贈之，小和尚得意之餘，貼在牆上，日日欣賞。左聯是「鳳棲禾下鳥飛去」，右聯是「馬走河邊草不生」。您知道這兩句謎題的謎底是什麼嗎？是「禿驢」！

→ 把鳳寫在「禾」下，將鳳字中的鳥拿掉變成「几」，豈不成了「禿」；河邊草是蘆葦，馬走到河邊，草都不生，把蘆字上的草去掉成了「盧」，再把「馬」字放旁邊，豈不是「驢」！

⑦ Q：When is a man like the letter B?（一個人何時像字母 **B**？）

　　A：When he is in bed.（當他就寢／在床上時。）

⑧ Q : What letter is an insect?（什麼字母是一隻昆蟲？）

A : B (Bee). 字母 B（〔蜜蜂〕。）

→ B 的發音與 Bee 同。

⑨ Q : What letter separates Europe from Africa?

（什麼字母將歐洲和非洲分開？）

A : C (sea).（字母 C〔海〕。）

→ sea 與 C 同音。

⑩ Q : Why is the letter D like a bad boy?（為何字母 D 像壞孩子？）

A : Because D makes ma mad.（因為 D 使媽瘋狂。）

→ d 加到 ma 後面就是 mad。

⑪ Q : What letter in the alphabet can travel the greatest distance?

（字母組中哪個字母能做最長路程的旅遊？）

A : The letter D, because it goes to the end of the world.

（字母 D，因為它能走到世界的盡頭。）

→ world 的末字為 d。

> 提起 the end of the world（世界末日）就會聯想起這首老情歌 *"The End of the World"* 歌詞極美，曲調悠揚，聽來令人柔腸寸斷。

⑫ Q : If all the letters of the alphabet were on top of a mountain, which letter would leave first?

（假設字母組的所有字母都在山頂，那個字會最先下山？）

A : D would always start descent.（下坡時字母 D 總是在開頭。）

→ descent 的第一個字母是 d。本題句型是假設語氣，與現在事實相反的假設語氣用過去式，由句中的 were 和 would 可看出。

⑬ Q : Why is making fun of people like the letter D on horseback?

（為何嘲弄人像字母 D 騎在馬背上？）

A : Because it is deriding (D riding).（因為它就是嘲笑〔D 騎馬〕。）

→ deriding 與 D riding 同音。

· **deride** [dı`raɪd] *v.* 嘲笑

14 Q : Why is the letter D like a sailor?（為何字母 **D** 像水手？）

　 A : Because it follows the C (sea).（因為它跟在 **C**〔海洋〕之後。）

15 Q : Why is the letter E like London?（為何字母 **E** 像倫敦？）

　 A : Because it is the capital of England.

　　　（因為它是英國的首都／**England** 的大寫。）

→ capital 亦作「大寫」解。

16 Q : Why is the letter E so unfortunate?（為何字母 **E** 如此不幸？）

　 A : Because it is always out of cash and always in debt and great
　　　danger.（因為 **E** 總是短缺現金且總是負債並在極度的危險之中。）

→ E 不在 cash 一字之內，而在 cash 之外。debt, great, danger 中都有字母 e。

17 Q : What is the most important thing in the world?

　　　（世界上最重要的東西是什麼？）

　 A : The letter E, because it is the first in everybody and everything.

　　　（字母 **E**，因為它在每個人和每件事的首位。）

→ e 在 everybody 和 everything 二字的第一個字母位置。這個謎題與第(11)題相似。

18 Q : Why is the letter F like death?（為何字母 **F** 像死亡？）

　 A : Because it makes all fall.（因為它使所有一切都倒下來。）

→ f 加 all 變為 fall。

19 Q : Why is the letter F like a cow's tail?（為何字母 **F** 像牛尾？）

　 A : Because it is at the end of beef.（因為它在牛肉的尾端。）

→ f 在 beef 的字尾。

20 Q : Why is the letter G like the sun?（為何字母 **G** 像太陽？）

　 A : Because it is the center of light.（因為 **G** 是光的中心。）

→ g 在 light 的中央。

㉑ Q：Why is I the happiest of the vowels?（為何 I 是母音中最幸福的？）

　A：Because it alone is in bliss, while E is in hell and all the other vowels are in purgatory.（因為只有 I 在無上幸福之中，而 E 在地獄裡，其他的母音〔A, O, U〕則在煉獄中。）

　　・ bliss [blɪs] *n.* 無上幸福，福祐，至福

　　・ hell [hɛl] *n.* 地獄

　　・ purgatory [ˋpɝgəˏtorɪ] *n.* 煉獄

㉒ Q：Why will one letter in the alphabet spell the word "potatoes"?

　　　（為何用一個字母即可拼成馬鈴薯一字？）

　A：The letter O. Put them down one at a time until you have put eight O's (potatoes).（字母 O。每次放下一個 O 直到放下八個 O〔馬鈴薯〕為止。）

　　→ put eight O's 與 potatoes 之發音相近。

㉓ Q：Why is the letter O like a pain?（為何字母 O 像痛苦？）

　A：Because it makes man moan.（因為它使人呻吟。）

　　→ o 加入 man 便成了 moan。

㉔ Q：Why is a false friend like the letter P?（為何偽友像字母 P？）

　A：Because he is the first in pity, but the last in help.

　　　（因為論「憐憫」他居前，但論「幫助」他最後。）

　　→ p 是 pity 的第一個字母，是 help 的最後一個字母。

㉕ Q：What is it that every pauper possesses that others have not?

　　　（每個貧民都擁有而其他人沒有的東西是什麼？）

　A：The letter P.（字母 P。）

　　→ 因 pauper 中有字母 p。

　　・ pauper [ˋpɔpɚ] *n.* 貧民

㉖ Q：Which two letters of the alphabet have nothing between them?

　　　（字母組中那兩個字母之間無任何東西？）

A：N and P have O (nothing) between them.（**N** 和 **P** 之間有字母 **O**。）

→ 這個字母 O 可看作是阿拉伯數字的 0。從 ...LMNOPQRS...，可看出 N 和 P 之間有一字母 O，像數字 0。

27 Q：Why is the letter R absolutely necessary to friendship?

（為何友誼中絕少不了字母 **R**？）

A：Without R, your friends would be fiends.

（沒有 **R**，你的朋友就變成了魔鬼。）

・**fiend** [find] *n.* 惡魔，…迷，…狂

例 He is a fresh air fiend.（他是一個最愛新鮮空氣的迷。）

28 Q：What letter is always invisible yet never out of sight?

（什麼字母總是看不見，但是卻不會不見？）

A：The letters I and S.（字母 **I** 和 **S**。）

→ invisible 跟 in visible 同音，i 和 s 在 visible 裡，卻也絕非在 sight 一字之外。

29 Q：Why are the letters C and S in the word "cloves", although separated, closely attached?

（字母 **C** 和 **S** 在丁香一字中雖然彼此分開，為何還是緊密的相連？）

A：Because there is love between them.（因為它們之間有愛。）

→ cloves 一字字首 c 和字尾 s 之間有 love。

・**cloves** [klov] *n.* 丁香

30 Q：What starts with a T, ends with a T, and is full of T?

（什麼東西開頭是 **T**，結尾是 **T**，而且全部都是 **T**？）

A：A teapot.（茶壺。）

→ teapot 的字首是 t，字尾是 t。teapot 裡裝的都是 t (tea)。

31 Q：What letter is a drink?（什麼字母是一種飲料？）

A：T (tea).（字母 **T**〔茶〕。）

→ tea，與 T 同音。

32 **Q**: Why is the letter T like an island?（為何字母 T 像一個島？）

　　A: Because it is in the midst of water.（因為它在水中央。）

　　→ water 中間的字母是 T。

T is like an island because it is in the midst of water.

33 **Q**: What letter will set one of the heavenly bodies in motion?

　　（什麼字母會使一個星體運動？）

　　A: T, because it will make a star start.（T，因為它使一顆星開始運動。）

　　→ t 加 star 變成 start。

34 **Q**: What letter makes pies inquisitive?（什麼字母使餡餅多問？）

　　A: The letter S will turn pies into spies.（字母 S 會將 pies 變成間諜。）

　　→ s 加 pies 變成 spies。

　　・inquisitive [ɪn`kwɪzətɪv] *adj.* 過分好問的，好追根究底的

　　例 Don't be so inquisitive!（不要打聽個沒完！）

35 **Q**: Why is U the jolliest letter?（為何 U 是最快樂的字母？）

　　A: Because it is always in the midst of fun.（因為它總是在樂趣之中。）

　　→ u 在 fun 一字的中央。

提到 fun 這個字，就聯想到一句諺語：

What is fun, isn't hard. What is hard, isn't fun.（趣事不難而難事無趣。）

還有一則有關 fun 的笑話：

一個兒子留學國外，不好好唸書，經常捎信給老爹要錢，但信卻越寫越短。

有一次寫信回來：

Dear Dad,

      No mon. No fun.

          Your son

他連 money 都懶得寫，簡寫成 mon。老爹讀信，也回了一信：

Dear son,

      So bad. So Sad.

          Your Dad

36 Q : When can the alphabet be shortened?（字母組何時可被縮短？）

A : When U and I are one.（當 U〔你〕和 I〔我〕成為一體時。）

37 Q : What letter is always nine inches long?（什麼字母總是 9 吋長？）

A : The letter Y, which is always one-fourth of a yard.

  （字母 Y，Y 是一碼的 4 分之 1。）

→ yard 有四個字母，y 占了 4 分之 1，合 9 吋長。因一碼等於 3 呎，1 呎等於 12 吋，

  1 碼等於 36 吋，4 分之 1 碼等於 9 吋。

38 Q : What letter is never found in the alphabet?

  （什麼字母／信件絕不會在字母組中找到？）

A : The one you mail.（你寄的那個字母／信件。）

→ letter 可作「字母」解，亦作「信」解。

39 Q : What four letters of the alphabet would scare off a burglar?

  （字母組中那四個字母會嚇走夜賊？）

A : O, I, C, U (Oh, I see you).（O, I, C, U〔哦，我看到你啦〕。）

40 Q : Which are the most sensible letters?（哪些字母最敏感？）

A : The Y's (wise).（字母 Y。）

→ 聰明，Y's 與 wise 同音。

41 Q : What letter is a part of the head?（什麼字母是頭的一部分？）

A : I (eye).（字母 I〔眼〕。）

→ I 與 eye 同音。

42 Q : What word of only three syllables contains twenty-six letters?

（什麼字僅有三個音節卻能包括二十六個字母？）

A : Alphabet.（字母組。）

· alphabet [ˋælfəˌbɛt] *n.* 字母組 (abc...xyz)

· syllable [ˋsɪləbl̩] *n.* 音節

43 Q : If all the letters of the alphabet were invited to a luncheon party, what six letters would fail to arrive on time?

（假設字母組中所有的字母都受邀參加午宴，哪六個字母無法準時到達？）

A : The letters U, V, W, X, Y and Z, because they come only after T (tea).（字母 U, V, W, X, Y 和 Z，因為只在 T〔茶會〕之後才到。）

44 Q : Why is a sewing machine like the letter S?（為什麼縫紉機像字母 S？）

A : Because it makes needles needless.（因為它使針變得無用。）

→ 將 s 加到 needles 後面變成 needless，needles 是 needle (針) 的複數，needless (無用的) 是由 need 加 less 而成。(注意 needles 與 needless 兩者發音不同。)

10 *What Is It?*

「什麼一旦失去就不可復得？」謎底是「時間 (time)」。「什麼東西越放久越年輕？」謎底是「肖像 (portrait)」。「什麼東西白天滿地跑，晚上靠牆角？」謎底是「掃帚 (broom)」。

現在讓我們來看看有關 **What is it?** 的謎題：

1 Q: What is it that has eyes but can't see?（什麼東西有眼睛卻無法看？）

A: A potato.（馬鈴薯。）

→ 馬鈴薯長出的小點稱為 eye。

2 Q: What is it that grows the more you take away from it?

（什麼東西你從中拿走越多它就變得越大？）

A: A hole.（洞。）

→ 洞越挖當然越大。

3 Q: What is it that everybody gives but few take?

（什麼東西人人給予但很少人接受？）

A: Advice.（忠告。）

例 I give him some good advice.（我給了他一些好意見。）
Please take my advice.（請接受我的勸告。）

4 Q: What is it that when once lost you can never find again?

（什麼東西失去就找不回來？）

A: Time.（時間。）

→ 時間一閃即逝，無從掌握，即

Time flashes through the present.

使短短的一秒，都無法握住，時間不斷的流逝，無人可擋。所以有一句諺語說得好：Time and tide wait for no man. (歲月不饒人。)

有句有關時間的話，值得回味：

Time comes from the past, flashes through the present and goes into the future. (時間來自過去，閃過現在而走向未來。)

另有一段有關時間的短文請參見附錄 C *(Present Past Future)*

⑤ Q: What is it that is always behind time? (什麼東西總是落在時間之後？)

A: The back of a watch. (錶背。)

→ 錶用來報時，錶背在錶的後面，當然是落在時間之後。事實上錶內是沒有時間的。請參見附錄 B2

⑥ Q: What is it that passes in front of the sun yet casts no shadow?

（什麼東西在太陽前面經過卻不投下影子？）

A: The wind. (風。)

有一篇描寫風的短文很美：

Who has seen the wind? (誰見過風？)

Neither you nor I. (既非你也非我。)

But when the trees bow down their heads, (但當樹彎下它們的樹梢時，)

The wind is passing by. (風正從旁通過。)

Who has seen the wind? (誰見過風？)

Neither I nor you. (既非我也非你。)

But when the leaves hang trembling, (但當樹葉掛著抖動時，)

The wind is passing through. (風正從中穿過。)

⑦ Q: What is it that is bought by the yard but worn by the foot?

（什麼東西論碼買進，但卻論呎損壞／被腳損壞？）

A: A carpet. (地毯。)

→ 腳在地毯上走，所以地毯被腳損壞，但 foot 亦作「呎」解。

買賣東西用什麼做單位要用 by 這個字。例：

The tea is sold by the pound. (茶葉論磅出售。)

The cloth is sold by the meter. (布論公尺出售。)

A thorn in your foot.

8 **Q**: Find it, ran home, look for it, found it, didn't want it and threw it away. What was it?

（發現了，跑回家，尋找它，找到了，不要它把它丟掉。是什麼東西？）

A: A thorn in my foot. (腳裡的刺。)

9 **Q**: What is it that has a tongue but cannot talk?

（什麼東西有舌頭卻不會說話？）

A: A shoe. (鞋子。)

→ 鞋面下的鞋舌稱為 tongue。

10 **Q**: What is it that has legs but can't walk? (什麼東西有腿但不會行走？)

A: A table or a chair. (桌子或椅子。)

→ 桌椅的腳叫 legs (腿)。

例 A table has four legs. (一張桌子有四隻腳。)

The leg of the table is broken. (桌腳斷了。)

11 **Q**: What is it that lives in winter, dies in summer, and grows with its roots upward? (什麼東西冬存夏亡，而根向上長？)

A: An icicle. (冰柱。)

12 **Q**: What is it that contains more feet in winter than in summer?

（什麼東西在冬天比在夏天有更多的腳？）

A: An outdoor skating rink. (戶外滑冰場。)

⑬ Q : What is it that you ought to keep after you have given it to someone else?（什麼東西在你給了別人之後，你仍應自己保存？）

A : A promise.（諾言。）

· **keep your promise** 遵守你的諾言

Keep your promise.

⑭ Q : What is it that everyone in the world is doing at the same time?（世界上每個人同時在做的是什麼？）

A : Growing old.（越來越老。）

⑮ Q : What is it that is always coming but never arrives?（什麼東西總正要到來，但從未來臨過？）

A : Tomorrow.（明天。）

→ 當明天來臨時已經是今天了。請參見附錄 D

⑯ Q : What is it that can be broken without being hit or dropped?（什麼東西不經打擊或掉落就可打破？）

A : Silence.（安靜。）

⑰ Q : What is it that you need most in the long run?（什麼東西終究是你最需要的？）

A : Your breath.（你的呼吸。）

· **in the long run** 畢竟，終究

提到 **breath**，有這樣一句諺語：
The first breath is the beginning of death.（第一口呼吸是死亡的開始。）
→ 這話說來似乎很悲觀，但深涵哲理，世上的事有開始就有結束，這是自然定律。

⑱ Q : What is it that everybody wants, and yet wants to get rid of as soon as possible?（什麼東西大家都想要，但卻想越快消除越好？）

A : A good appetite.（好胃口。）

→ 在德國，在用餐前，對共餐者會說：" Good appetite!" 這是德國人的餐桌禮節。

⑲ **Q** : What is it that works when it plays and plays when it is working?

（什麼東西在遊戲時工作，在工作時遊戲？）

A : A fountain.（噴泉。）

→ 噴泉在噴水時稱 "It plays."。

⑳ **Q** : What is it that can and does speak in every known language and yet never went to school?

（什麼東西能夠而且能確切的說每一種現有的語言卻從沒有上過學？）

A : An echo.（回音。）

→ 你對著峭壁大聲說話，傳回來的聲音(即回音)也跟你說的是同一語言。

㉑ **Q** : What is it that is always cracked when it is heard?

（什麼東西當被聽到時總是碎裂的？）

A : A joke.（笑話。）

· to crack a joke; to tell a joke 說笑話

A joke is cracked.

22 **Q**: What is it that will go up a chimney down, but won't go down the chimney up?（什麼東西穿煙囱而上時向下，而當它向上時無法穿煙囱而下？）

A: An umbrella.（雨傘。）

→ 這題要仔細思索，傘撐開時，我們說 "It is up." 傘收攏時，我們說 "It is down." 所以當傘在 down 時，可穿煙囱而上；傘在 up 時，無法穿煙囱而下。

23 **Q**: What is it that has two heads, six feet, one tail and four ears?

（什麼東西有兩個頭，六隻腳，一條尾巴和四個耳朵？）

A: A man on horse back.（一個人騎在馬背上。）

24 **Q**: What is it that you cannot see, but is always before you?

（什麼東西你看不見，但總是在你面前？）

A: The future.（將來。）

> The past cannot be caught, nor can the future be reached. The present is the most reliable.（過去抓不回，未來探不到，只有現在最可靠。）
>
> 請參見附錄 C、D

25 **Q**: What is it that never has anything to say, but its action is always directly to the point?（什麼東西從不說什麼，但它的行動總是針對要點？）

A: A wasp.（黃蜂。）

26 **Q**: What is it that though dark has done most to enlighten the world?

（什麼東西雖然暗，卻曾做過很多照亮世界的工作／啟迪世界的工作？）

A : Ink. (墨汁。)

→ 題中的 enlighten 亦作「教化」解。

㉗ **Q** : What is it that always walks with its head downward?

（什麼東西走路時總是垂著頭？）

A : A nail in your shoe. (鞋底的釘子。)

㉘ **Q** : What is it that while it is yours alone, is used much more by other people than by yourself?

（有一樣東西是你的，別人卻用的比你多，是什麼？）

A : Your name. (你的名字。)

㉙ **Q** : What is it that goes around the house in daytime and lies in a corner at night? （什麼東西白天滿屋跑，晚上靠牆角？）

A : A broom. (掃帚。)

㉚ **Q** : What is it that becomes younger the longer it exists?

（什麼東西越放久越年輕？）

A : A portrait of a person. (肖像。)

→ 像放越久越年輕，現在看廿年前的像跟十年後再看同一張像當然感覺不一樣。

㉛ **Q** : What is it that we never borrow but often return?

（什麼東西我們從不借來，但常要還回去？）

A : Thanks. (謝謝。)

㉜ **Q** : What is it that grows longer the more it is cut?

（什麼東西切除得越多就變得越長？）

A : A ditch. (水溝。)

→ 水溝越挖越長。

㉝ **Q** : What is it that has eight feet and can sing?

（什麼東西有八隻腳且能唱歌？）

A : A quartet. (四重唱。)

→ 四人組合而成的，故有八隻腳。

34 Q: What is it that we have in December that we don't have in any other month?（什麼東西我們在十二月裡才有，其他月份裡沒有？）

A: The letter D.（字母 D。）

→ 我們將十二個月寫出來看看：January, February, March, April, May, June, July, August, September, October, November, December。十二個月份中沒有 k, q, w, x 和 z。

35 Q: What is it that has eighteen legs and catches flies?

（什麼東西有十八條腿，並能捉蒼蠅／飛球？）

A: A baseball team.（棒球隊。）

→ 一支棒球隊有九名球員：投手，捕手，一、二、三壘手，左、右外野手，兩個游擊手。

36 Q: What is it that stays hot in a refrigerator?

（什麼東西放在冰箱裡還是熱的／辣的？）

A: Mustard.（芥菜。）

→ hot 亦作「辣」解。吃了辣椒會說："Oh! It's hot!"

37 Q: What is it that runs in and out of town all day and night?

（什麼東西白天和晚上都往城裡跑進跑出？）

A: The road.（道路。）

38 Q: What is it that everyone can divide, but no one can see the place at which it has been divided?

（什麼東西每個人都能把它分開，但無人能看到被分開的地方？）

A: Water.（水。）

39 Q: What is it that goes up and never goes down?

（什麼東西一直增加而絕不減少？）

A: Your age.（你的年齡。）

40 Q : What is it that goes farther the slower it goes?

（什麼東西走得越慢就走得越遠？）

A : Your money.（你的錢。）

→ 錢慢慢的用，就能用得久。此即細水長流的道理。

Money goes farther the slower it goes.

11 *How's Your Geography?*

地理 (geography) 怎麼會跟謎語有關？這是個有趣的問題，答案就在以下的英文謎題中，但在猜英文謎之前，先看看中國的謎題，請看以下兩個對句：

「天寒地凍，水無一點不成冰。國破家亡，王不出頭誰作主？」請看「冰」字，是不是「水」加一「點」；「主」是不是把「王」弄出「頭」來。國字很妙，再看兩句：「凍窗洒雨，東兩滴西三滴。切瓜分片，橫七刀豎八刀。」「東」加兩「滴」就成了「凍」；「西」加三「滴」就成了「洒」。

現在就讓我們來看看有關 **geography** 的謎題：

①Q: Can you make sense of the following:（你能解出以下所列的意義嗎？）

Yy Ur yy Ub

I C U r yy 4 me.

A: Too wise you are, too wise you be, I see you are too wise for me.

（你太聰明，你夠聰明，我知道對我來講你是夠聰明的。）

→ 兩個 Y 寫在一起 YY 唸成 "two Y's"，與 "too wise" 同音。4 (four) 與 for 音相近。

②Q: Can you make the following sense:（你能使下列的字有意義嗎？）

stand	take	to	world
I	you	throw	the

A: I understand you undertake to overthrow the underworld.

（我知道你承擔起推翻下流社會的責任。）

→ I 在 stand 之下，故為 I understand；to 在 throw 之上，故為 to overthrow；其餘類推。

③Q: How can you make sense out of the following sentence: "It was and I said not but?"（你如何使下列的句子具有意義：「如文」。）

A : "It was AND, I said, not BUT." (「我說它是 **AND**，不是 **BUT**。」)

4 Q : Write down VOLIX, and ask a friend how to pronounce it.

（寫下 **VOLIX**，問一個朋友如何讀法。）

A : Volume nine (Vol. IX). （第九卷〔**Vol. IX**〕。）

5 Q : How can you make fifteen barrels of corn from one barrel?

（你如何能用一桶玉米製成十五桶？）

A : By popping it. （焙珠／即將它爆成爆米花。）

· popcorn [ˋpɑpˌkɔrn] *n.* 爆米花

Popping the corn.

6 Q : How might you be completely sleepless for seven days and still not lack any rest? （如何才能七天不睡而仍不會缺乏休息？）

A : By sleeping nights. （在晚上睡覺就好了。）

→ 題中只問 seven days，未說 "Seven days and nights." day，天，亦作「白天」解。

7 Q : What relation is that child to its father who is not its father's own son? （如果那個孩子不是他父親自己的兒子，則與他父親的關係是什麼？）

A : His daughter. （他的女兒。）

8 **Q**: Name a carpenter's tool you can spell forward and backward the same way. （列出一件木匠的工具名字，順唸或倒唸都一樣。）

A: Level.（水平儀。）

9 **Q**: Under what circumstances are a builder and a newspaper reporter equally likely to fail?（在何種情況下建築工和新聞記者同樣可能遭到失敗？）

A: When they make up stories without foundations.

（當他們建屋而不打地基時／當他們編故事而無根據時。）

10 **Q**: Two Indians are standing on a hill, and one is the father of the other's son. What relations are the two Indians to each other?

（兩個印第安人站在山丘上，其中一個是另一個兒子的父親。這兩個印第安人彼此之間的關係是什麼？）

A: Husband and wife.（夫妻。）

11 **Q**: How can you divide seven apples absolutely equally among eleven small boys?（你如何把七個蘋果完全地平分給十一個小孩？）

A: Make the apples into apple sauce, and measure it out very carefully.（把蘋果做成蘋果醬，小心的量一量。）

12 **Q**: If a carpenter receives twenty-five cents for sawing a board into two lengths, how much should he receive for sawing the board into four lengths?（如果一個木匠把一塊木板鋸成兩截收費兩角五分，將一塊木板鋸成四截收費多少？）

A: Seventy-five cents, because it takes only three saw-cuts.

（七角五分，因為只須鋸三下。）

13 **Q**: There are sixteen ears of corn in a barrel. A rabbit came each night and carried away three ears. How long did it take him to empty the barrel?（一個桶裡裝了十六個玉蜀黍的穗〔耳朵〕，一隻兔子每晚含走三支穗〔耳朵〕，需要多久地才能把桶搬空？）

A : It takes him sixteen nights, because each night he carried away one ear of corn and his own two ears. This made three ears each night. （需要十六夜，因為兔子每晚帶走一個玉蜀黍穗〔耳朵〕加上自己的兩隻耳朵。這樣每晚才帶走三隻耳朵。）

14 Q : Marven bet that he could eat more oysters than Barnet. Marven ate ninety in a week, and Barnet ate a hundred and one. How many more did Barnet eat than Marven? （馬文打賭吃蠔比巴尼多。馬文一星期吃了九十個，而巴尼吃了一百零一個，巴尼比馬文多吃幾個？）

A : Ten. He ate a hundred and won (one).

（多吃十個。巴尼吃了一百個而贏了。）

→ 此處 won 與 one 同音。

15 Q : There is a girl in a candy store in Denver who is 6 feet 6 inches tall, has a waist measure of 42 inches, and wears number 12 shoes. What do you think she weighs?

（在丹佛一家糖果店裡，一個女孩身高 6 呎 6 吋，腰圍 42 吋，穿 12 號鞋，你認為她體重多少／你認為她在秤什麼？）

A : She weighs candy. （她在秤糖果。）

→ weigh 亦作「秤」解。

She weights candy.

12 *Girls Are Always Riddles*

「女子」二字合在一起寫就成了「好」。所以女子常被用來做比喻 (metaphor)，例如「一輪明月」常以「像一張睡著的美人的臉」來形容。有時形容天氣陰雨難測，則用「小姐的脾氣」。

現在讓我們來看看有關 **Girls** 的謎題：

① **Q** : When is a pretty girl like a ship?（何時漂亮的女孩子像船？）

A : When she's attached to a boy (buoy).（當她依附著男孩時〔繫浮標時〕。）

→ boy 與 buoy 同音。

· **buoy** [bɔɪ] *n.* 浮標，航標

· **be attached to**　附著；愛

例 He is attached to his son.（他愛他的兒子。）

② **Q** : How can a girl best keep a boy's affection?

（一個女孩子如何才能保有男孩子的愛情？）

A : By not returning it.（不要還以愛情。）

③ **Q** : How would it work if all the post offices were in the charge of pretty girls?（假設郵局由美麗的女孩子負責管理，營運將如何？）

A : It would work so well that the mails (males) would arrive and depart every hour of the day.

（工作會非常順利，郵件〔男性〕會在一天中每小時有來往。）

→ male (男性) 與 mail (郵件) 同音。

④ **Q** : If a girl fell into a well, why wouldn't her brother help her out?

（如果一個女孩子掉到井裡，為何她的兄弟不把救她出來？）

A : How could he be a brother and assist her (a sister) too?

（他怎能身為兄弟又去幫她呢／他怎麼能夠既是兄弟又是姊妹呢？）

→ assist her (幫助她) 與 a sister (一個姊妹) 發音相似。

⑤ Q：In what month do girls talk the least?（在哪個月裡女孩子說話最少？）

A：In February, because it is the shortest month.

（在二月裡，因為二月最短。）

→ 二月僅 28 天。閏年多一天，29 天。有一首有關閏年 (*leap year*) 的詩。請參見附錄 E

⑥ Q：How can you tell a girl named Ellen that she is delightful, in eight letters?（你如何用八個字母告訴名叫愛倫的女孩子她很開朗悅人？）

A：URABUTLN. (You are a beauty, Ellen.)

（順著字母唸下去就是：「你是個美人，愛倫。」）

⑦ Q：What is the difference between a soldier and a pretty girl?

（士兵和漂亮的女孩子有何差異？）

A：One faces the powder, and the other powders the face.

（前者面對火藥，而後者把火藥／香粉撲在臉上。）

女士想上洗手間，可用 "I want to powder my nose." 這句話可別譯成「我想把粉撲在鼻子上」。

⑧ Q：Why is a nice but inelegant girl like brown sugar?

（為何一個美麗但不高雅的女孩子像黃砂糖？）

A：Because she is sweet but unrefined.（她很甜但未經提煉。）

→ unrefined 亦作「不高雅」解。

・**refined** [rɪˋfaɪnd] *adj.* 提煉的

⑨ Q：Why is a proud girl like a music book?（為何驕傲的女孩子像音樂書本？）

A：Because she is full of airs.（因為她盡擺架子／充滿了曲調。）

・**put on airs** 裝腔作勢

例 He put on airs with his learning.（他因有學問而裝腔作勢。）

⑩ Q：Why do girls make good post-office clerks?

（為何女孩子能當好的郵局人員？）

A : Because they know how to manage the mails (males).

（因為她們知道如何處理信件〔對付男性〕。）

→ mails (信件) 與 males (男性) 同音。

· **female** [`fimel] *n.* 女性

⑪ **Q** : Why should not girls learn foreign language?

（為何女孩子不該學外國語言？）

A : Because one tongue is enough for a girl.

（因為對任何一個女孩子而言，一個舌頭〔語言〕已經夠了。）

→ tongue 亦作「語言」解。例：mother tongue (母語)。

這題的謎底亦可譯為「對女孩子而言，一種語言已經足夠了。」故毋需學習外國語言，她只需母語就夠了。

One tongue is enough for a girl.

⑫ **Q** : Why are some girls like fact?（為何有些女孩子像事實？）

A : Because they are stubborn things.

（因為她們是不容打消的事情／是倔強的東西。）

· stubborn [ˋstʌbɚn] *adj.* 倔強的

⑬ Q：Why are some girls like salad?（為何有些女孩子像沙拉？）

A：Because they need a lot of dressing.

（因為沙拉需要很多調味料／女孩子需要很多衣物。）

⑭ Q：Why is a bright girl's thought like the E-mail?

（為何一個聰明女孩子的觀念像電子郵件？）

A：Because it's so much quicker than the mail (male) intelligence.

（因為它比郵件傳送快得多／比男士的智慧快得多。）

> male 與 mail 同音，有關這兩個字的謎題很多，讀者可慢慢欣賞。

⑮ Q：When is a girl not a girl?（女孩子何時不是女孩子？）

A：When she is a bell (belle) or a deer (dear).

（當她是一座鐘〔美人〕或一隻鹿〔親愛的〕時。）

→ bell (鐘) 與 belle (美人) 同音；deer (鹿) 與 dear (親愛的) 同音。

⑯ Q：When is a girl's cheek not a cheek?（女孩子的臉頰何時不是臉頰？）

A：When it is a little pail (pale).（當它是一個小桶〔蒼白〕時。）

→ pail (小桶) 與 pale (蒼白的) 同音。

⑰ Q：Why are girls like hinges?（為何女孩子像門的樞紐？）

A：Because they are things to a door (adore).

（因為她們是用之於門的東西〔受人愛慕的〕。）

→ a door (一扇門) 與 adore (愛慕的) 同音。

⑱ Q：What girl is always making blinders?（什麼女孩總是犯錯？）

A：Miss Take (mistake).（**Take** 小姐〔錯誤〕。）

→ Miss Take (Take 小姐) 與 mistake (錯誤) 同音。

19 Q : What is the difference between a girl and a parasol?

（女孩子與女用陽傘有何不同？）

A : You can shut up the parasol.（你能把陽傘收合起來。）

→ 女孩子話匣子一開，就像關不住的水龍頭，難以 shut up。

・shut up 閉嘴

You can shut up the parasol.

20 Q : Why is a melancholy girl the most pleasant of all companions?

（為何一個憂鬱的女孩子是最快樂的同伴？）

A : Because she is always a-musing (amusing).

（因為她總是沉思的〔快樂的〕。）

→ muse (沉思)，amusing (快樂的) 同音。

21 Q : Why should girls always set a good example?

（為何女孩子總應該樹立一個好榜樣？）

A : Because boys are so apt to follow them.

（因為男孩子很容易仿效她們／跟在後面。）

→ follow 可作「跟在…之後」解，亦可作「仿效」解。

22 Q : Why are girls so extravagant about their clothes?

（為何女孩子對她們的衣服如此浪費？）

A : Because when they get a new dress, they wear it out the first day.

（因為當她們有了一件新衣服時，她們當天就把它穿破／穿出去了。）

→ wear it out 字譯為「把它穿出去」，亦作「穿破」或「穿舊」解。

· worn out 疲困的 = very tired 極為疲倦

例 I am worn out.（我很疲倦。）切不可字譯為「我被穿出去。」

· wear [wɛr] *v.* (wear/ wore/ worn) 穿

23 Q : When is a girl not sorry to lose her hair?

（何時女孩子掉了頭髮也不會難過？）

A : When she has it cut.（當她叫人把它剪掉的時候。）

· cut [kʌt] *v.* (cut/ cut/ cut) 切，剪，割

例 She has her hair cut.（她叫人剪她的頭髮。）→ 句中的 cut 為過去分詞。

She cut her hair.（她過去剪她的頭髮。）

She cuts her hair every day.（她每天剪她的頭髮。）

She has him cut her hair.（她叫他剪她的頭髮。）→ 句中的 cut 為原形動詞。

24 Q : Why is a fashionable school for girls like a flower garden?

（為何一所時髦的／貴族的女子學校像一座花園？）

A : Because it is a place of haughty culture (horticulture).

（因為它是傲慢之處〔園藝術〕。）

→ haughty culture 與 horticulture 發音相近。

· haughty [`hɔtɪ] *adj.* 傲慢的、驕傲的，不遜的

· culture [`kʌltʃɚ] *n.* 文化

· horticulture [`hɔrtɪˌkʌltʃɚ] *n.* 園藝學，造園

25 Q : If there were only three girls in the world, what do you think they would talk about?（假設世界上只有三個女孩子，你想她們會談些什麼？）

A : Two of them would get together and talk about the other one.

（其中兩個會聚在一起談論另外一個。）

> 國字的會意字是很有趣的，「忘」是亡了心，沒有心，當然是忘記。「女子」寫在一起就成了「好」。「少女」為「妙」。三個女寫在一起就不是一個好字眼。這題的意思是說三個女人在一起就會有是非。

26 Q : What girls are they whose days are always unlucky?

（哪些女孩子的日子總是不幸福的？）

A : Miss Chance, Miss Fortune and Miss Hap.

（Cance 小姐，Fortune 小姐和 Hap 小姐）

> 壞運 (mischance)，災禍 (misfortune) 和不幸之事 (misshap)。
> Miss Chance（機會小姐）與 mischance（壞運）同音。
> Miss Fortune（財富小姐）與 misfortune（災禍）同音。
> Miss Hap（偶然小姐）與 misshap（不幸之事）同音。

27 Q : What are the three quickest ways of spreading the news?

（傳佈消息最快的三種方法是什麼？）

A : E-mail, telephone and tell a girl.（電子郵件，電話和告訴女孩子。）

> 小姐女士們讀到這個謎題，請勿見怪，此一妙答想必中外皆同。

28 Q : Why should a group of pretty girls squeezing wet clothes remind us of going to church?

（為何一群正在擰溼衣服的漂亮女孩能提醒我們上教堂？）

A : Because the belles (bells) are wringing (ringing).

（因為美人們〔鐘〕正在擰衣服〔正在響〕。）

→ belle (美人) 與 bell (鐘) 同音，wringing (擰衣服) 與 ringing (正在響) 同音。

・ wring [rɪŋ] *v.* 擰

・ ring [rɪŋ] *v.* (ring/ rang/ rung) 響

㉙ Q : What is the best way to find a mysterious girl out?

（把一個神祕的女孩子找出來的最好方法是什麼？）

A : Go around to her house when she isn't in.

（當她不在家時，到她家附近走走。）

→ You find her out. (你發現她外出。) 這句話也可解為「你把她找出來」。

find [faɪnd] *v.* (find/ found/ found) 發現，找到，發覺，感覺到

這個字常被用錯，請看以下例句：

1. I found a bee in the hive. (我在蜂窩裡發現一隻蜜蜂。)

2. They found the lost child hiding in the cave.

（他們發現失蹤的孩子躲在山洞裡。）

3. Can you find your way home? (你能找到回家的路嗎？)

4. I woke up to find myself in the hospital. (我醒來時發覺自己在醫院裡。)

5. I find it difficult to believe you. (我覺得很難相信你。)

「我正在找一位英文老師。」是 "I am looking for an English teacher." 而不是

"I am finding an English teacher." 請看下一句：

1. "I am just like a baby in darkness searching for a light switch that does
   not exist." (我只是像一個在黑暗中的嬰孩尋找一個不存在的電燈開關。)

2. "Those who foolishly sought power by riding the back of the tiger
   ended up inside." (那些傻傻騎在虎背上尋找權力的人最後進了虎肚。)

——甘迺迪總統就職演說詞

13 Animal Crackers

crackers 為餅乾，將餅乾做成各種動物的形狀，稱為 animal crackers。這裡所指的是以動物為主的文字遊戲或謎題。最通俗有關動物的中文謎題是「一家有七口，種田有一畝，還養一條狗（犬）。」猜一字，謎底是「獸」。英文謎題多用同音異義字，或同字異義字。例如：「什麼動物都在合法的文件上？」謎底是 "seal"（海豹），所指的是印章 (seal)，合法文件上要蓋 seal（印章），這就是同音異義字。

現在讓我們來看看有關 Animal Crackers 的謎題：

1 Q: Which animal is the heaviest in all creation?

（在所有生物中那一種動物最重？）

A: A led (lead) horse.（嚮導〔鉛〕馬。）

→ lead horse 鉛馬 (用鉛做的馬)，當然最重。led horse 嚮導馬 (led 是 lead 的過去分詞) leaded 是 lead 的過去式和過去分詞，加鉛了的。lead 當動詞用時是「加鉛」；例如：It is leaded. (它被加了鉛。)

· lead [lɛd] *n.* 鉛；*v.* 加鉛

· lead [lid] *v.* (lead/ led/ led) 引領

> unleaded（未被加鉛的）所以「無鉛汽油」就是 "unleaded gasoline"。加油站上面標示的無鉛汽油就是 "unleaded" 這個字。

2 Q: What animal is in every baseball game?（什麼動物在每場棒球比賽裡？）

A: A bat.（蝙蝠。）

→ 亦作「球棒」解。bat man 譯成「蝙蝠俠」。有 bat 這個字，是否有 bet？

· bet [bɛt] *n. v.* 打賭

· bit [bɪt] *n.* 一點點

· but [bʌt] *conj.* 但是

> 沒有 bot 這個字，但大寫的 BOT 是代表 Build Operation Transportation。五個母音 a、e、i、o、u 都用上了。

3 Q: What animal needs clothing, poor thing?

（什麼動物需要衣服，可憐的東西？）

A: Bear (bare). （熊〔赤裸裸的〕。）

→ bear 與 bare 同音。

4 Q: What animal never plays fair?（什麼動物從不公正無欺？）

A: Cheetah (cheater). （獵豹〔騙子〕。）

→ cheetah 與 cheater 音相近。

5 Q: What animal is nearest to your brain?（什麼動物最靠近你的頭腦？）

A: Hare (hair). （野兔〔頭髮〕。）

→ 二者同音。

Hare (hair) is nearest to your brain.

6 Q: What animal do you need when you are driving a car?

（什麼動物在你開車時需要牠？）

A: A good steer. （一頭好公牛／一個好駕駛。）

→ 此謎題是同字異義字。

· steer [stɪr] *n.* 公牛；駕駛

7 **Q**：What animal is your girl friend?（什麼動物是你的女朋友？）

A：Deer (dear).（鹿〔親愛的〕。）

→ deer (鹿) 與 dear (親愛的) 同音。

8 **Q**：When is a donkey spelled with one letter?

（驢子何時可用一個字母拼成？）

A：When it's U, dear.（當它是你〔**you**〕，親愛的。）

→ 這個妙答有些捉弄人。donkey 亦作「蠢人」解。

9 **Q**：What two animals go with you everywhere?

（那兩種動物跟著你到處走？）

A：Your calves.（小海豹／你的小腿。）

10 **Q**：What animals do you find in the clouds?（什麼動物可以在雲中找到？）

A：Reindeer (rain, dear).（馴鹿〔雨，親愛的〕。）

→ reindeer 與 rain, dear 同音。

11 **Q**：What farm animal is very much like a cannibal?

（什麼農莊動物很像食人者？）

A：A cow, because it always wants to eat its fodder (father).

（乳牛，因為牠總想吃牠的糧草〔父親〕。）

→ fodder 與 father 音相近。

· fodder [ˋfɑdɚ] *n.* 糧草

· father [ˋfɑðɚ] *n.* 父親

12 **Q**：What animal is on every legal document?

（什麼動物在每一件合法的文件上？）

A：A seal.（海豹／印章。）

→ 此題為同字異義字。

· seal [sil] *n.* 海豹；印章

13 Q：What animal would you like to be on a very cold day?

（在冷天裡，你喜歡當什麼動物？）

A：A little otter (hotter). （小水獺〔稍稍熱一點〕。）

→ a little otter 與 a little hotter 讀音相近。

14 Horse Laughs

　　在國畫中，馬是繪畫的題材之一；在成語故事裡，馬也有相當的分量。例如：塞翁失馬，青梅竹馬，走馬看花，老馬識途，馬馬虎虎等。在謎語中，最常見的謎題是「什麼馬不能騎？」謎底是「羅馬」或「巴拿馬」。

　　現在讓我們來看看有關 **Horse Laughs** 的謎語：

1️⃣ Q：How can you make a slow horse fast?（如何使一匹慢馬加快／絕食？）

A：Don't give him anything to eat for a while.

　　（一段時間不給牠任何東西吃。）

→ fast 亦作「絕食」、「齋戒」解。古代英國有某些人守齋戒 (fast)，早晨是不吃東西的，若有人不守戒律，早晨吃了東西，那就破 (break) 戒 (fast) 了，於是 breakfast 就成了早餐。

2️⃣ Q：How can you put a good horse on his mettle?（如何使一匹馬奮勇？）

A：Shoe him. That will put him on his metal.

　　（替牠釘上蹄釘。那才能將鐵蹄釘在牠的腳上。）

→ on his metal 與 on his mettle 讀音相同。

　例 We put him on his mettle.（我們使他奮起。）

・ mettle [ˋmɛtl̩] *n.* 勇氣

・ put one on one's mettle　使人奮起

3️⃣ Q：Why is a horse like the letter O?（為何馬像字母 O？）

A：Because gee (g) makes it go.（因為噓聲能使馬向前走。）

→ g 加 o 即成 go。

4️⃣ Q：Why is a wild young horse like an egg?（為何小野馬像蛋？）

A：It must be broken before it can be used.

　　（因為蛋在使用／食用之前必須把它打破。）

→ 小馬在使用之前必須是馴服的。broken 作「馴服的」解。broken 為打破 (break) 之過去分詞。

5 **Q** : Why is a well-trained horse like a kind hearted man?

（為何一隻訓練有素的馬像一位仁慈的人？）

A : Because he always stops at the sound of whoa (woe).

（因為他聽到停止〔悲哀〕的叫聲就停下來。）

→ whoa [hwo] *int.* 與 woe 同音。

· whoa [hwo] *int.* 令馬停下來的叫聲

· woe [wo] *n.* 悲傷，哀愁

例 We will be leaving at 6 o'clock sharp, and woe betide anyone who is late.

（我們將在六點整出發，誰遲到誰倒霉。）

6 **Q** : Why does tying a slow horse to a post make him a better racer?

（為何繫慢馬於柱上使他成為一匹好賽馬？）

A : Because it makes him fast.（因為那將使他跑的快。）

· make...fast 將…繫於柱子上

例 We make the boat fast.（我們繫船於柱上。）

7 **Q:** Why is even a good-natured hunting horse likely to get angry unexpectedly?（即使是一匹本性善良的獵馬為何可能會不期然地發怒？）

A: Because the better tempered he is, the easier he takes a fence.

（因為牠的脾氣越好，就越容易令牠進欄。）

→ take a fence (進欄) 與 take offense (動怒) 讀音相近。

8 **Q:** How can it be proved that a horse has six legs?

（如何能證明一隻馬有六條腿？）

A: Because he has fore legs (four legs) in front and two legs behind.

（因為牠有前腿〔四條腿〕在前和兩條腿在後。）

→ forelegs (前腿) 和 four legs (四條腿) 同音。

9 **Q:** What do you think is the principal part of a horse?

（你認為馬的主要部分是什麼？）

A: His mane (main) part.（牠的馬鬃〔主要〕部分。）

→ main [men] (主要的) 與 mane (馬鬃) 同音。

The prineipal part of a horse is the mane (main) part.

15 See Any Resemblances?

"See any resemblances?"（看到有何相似之處？）從兩個字的動詞三態變化可以造出一個謎題來：「為何擦鞋匠和太陽相似？」這是因為擦亮是 shine，太陽照耀也是這個 shine。

現在讓我們來看看相關的謎題：

1 **Q**: Why does a bootblack resemble the sun?（為何擦鞋匠和太陽相似？）

A: Because he shines for all.（因為他為大家擦鞋／普照萬物。）

→ 同樣是 shine，但意義不同，此即同字異義字。

· shine [ʃaɪn] *v.* (shine/ shined/ shined) 擦亮
· shine [ʃaɪn] *v.* (shine/ shone/ shone) 照耀

例 He shines his shoes every day.（他每天擦他的鞋子。）

　The sun shines for all.（太陽普照萬物。）

2 **Q**: Why does a good gardener resemble a detective-story writer?

　（為何好的園丁和偵探故事的作者相似？）

A: Because he works hard at his plot.

　（因為園丁努力於田園工作／作者努力寫劇中情節。）

· plot [plɑt] *n.* 小塊土地，情節

例 The plot was so complicated that I couldn't follow it.

　（情節如此複雜，以致於我都無法了解。）

　He grew potatoes on his little plot of land.

　（他在他的一塊小土地上種馬鈴薯。）

3 **Q**: Why does a hat resemble a king?（為何帽子和國王相似？）

A: Because it has a crown.（因為帽子有帽頂／國王有王冠。）

4 **Q**: Why do laws resemble the ocean?（為何法律和海洋相似？）

A : Because the most trouble is caused by the breaker.

（因為大部分的困擾皆由破壞者而引起／碎浪所造成。）

· breaker [`brekɚ] *n.* （沖擊岸邊岩上的）碎浪；破壞者

例 I see breaker on the shore. （我看到海岸邊的碎浪。）

He is a law-breaker. （他是犯法者。）

> breaker 是由現在式的 break 加 er 而成，那麼過去式 broke 加 er 而成的 broker 是什麼？答案是「仲介」。

⑤ Q : Why does opening a letter resemble a strange way of entering a room? （為何開信和用奇怪的方式進入房間相似？）

A : Because it is breaking through the ceiling (sealing).

（因為它要穿過天花板〔經過拆封〕。）

→ 信封的封口為 sealing，與 ceiling (天花板) 同音。

· seal [sil] *n.* 印章

⑥ Q : Why does a young man trying to raise a moustache resemble a cow's tail? （為何年輕人蓄唇鬍和牛尾相似？）

A : Because he is growing down. （因為它是向下長的。）

→ 牛尾和唇鬍都是向下長。

· grow up 向上長，長大

例 He is growing up. （他長大。）

⑦ Q : Why does a love of the ocean resemble curiosity?

（為何愛好海洋和好奇相似？）

A : Because it has sent many a boy to sea (see).

（因為它把很多男孩送往海洋〔吸引很多男孩去觀看〕。）

· curiosity [kjʊrɪ`ɑsətɪ] *n.* 好奇心

· curious [`kjʊrɪəs] *adj.* 好奇的

例 We were curious to know where she had gone. （我們很好奇她去了哪裡。）

I have an intense curiosity about their plan.

（我對他們的計畫有強烈的好奇心。）

8 Q : Why does a farmer guiding a plow resemble an ocean liner?（為何掌犁的農夫和遠洋海輪相似？）

A : Because one sees the plow, and the other plows the sea.

（因為前者可看到耕田的犁，後者在海上破浪前進。）

The farmer sees the plow.

· **plow; plough** [plaʊ] *n.* 犁 *v.* 犁田

例 In some countries, ploughs are pulled by oxen.（在有些國家，犁用牛來拉。）

Farmers plough in spring.（農夫春天犁田。）

The ship ploughed across the ocean.（這艘船在海洋中破浪前進。）

An ocean liner plows the sea.

9 Q : Why does a postage stamp resemble an obstinate donkey?

（為何一張郵票和一隻倔強的驢子相似？）

A : Because the more you lick it the more it sticks.

（因為舔〔背面塗有膠水的郵票〕得越多則黏得越緊／打得越多則驢子越僵〔驢子脾氣一發則越打越不聽話〕。）

· lick [lɪk] *v.* 舔

· stick [stɪk] *v.* (stick/ stuck/ stuck) 黏住

· lick an ice cream 舔吃冰淇淋

· lick one's wound 重整旗鼓，重新積蓄力量

10 Q : Why does a pig in a parlor resemble a fire?

（為何豬欄裡的豬和失火相似？）

A : Because the sooner it is put out the better.

（因為趕出會客室越早越好／撲滅得越快越好。）

· parlor, parlour [ˋpɑrlɚ] *n.* 店；會客室；客廳

· put out 撲滅

例 The fire is put out.（火被撲滅。）

11 Q : Why does a New Year's resolution resemble an egg?

（為何新年立的願和蛋相似？）

A : Because it is so easily broken.（因為容易打破。）

→ 國外習俗，每逢新年，必立一願，譬如戒煙，戒酒或戒牌。但過不多久，故態復萌，所以說 "It is so easily broken."。

12 Q : Why do sentries resemble day and night?（為何哨兵和晝夜相似？）

A : Because when one comes the other goes.（因為一個來另一個走。）

→ 因為白天去了夜晚就隨即來到。一個哨兵下更，另一個隨即上更。哨兵站哨有一定的時間，時間到了另一個就會來換班。一個去另一個來，跟晝去夜來一樣。

13 Q : Why do the fixed stars resemble paper?（為何固定的星星和紙相似？）

A : Because they are stationary (stationery).

（因為它們是固定不動的〔文具〕。）

→ 二字只是一字之差，固定的是 "a"，文具是 "e"。

- stationary [`steʃən,ɛrɪ] *adj.* 固定的
- stationery [`steʃən,ɛrɪ] *n.* 文具

⑭ Q : Why does your shadow resemble a false friend?

（為何你的身影和偽友相似？）

A : Because it only follows you in sunshine, and desert you when you are under a cloud.

（因為他僅在陽光下／在你好運時跟隨你，在雲層下／在你倒霉時離開你。）

- shadow [`ʃædo] *n.* 影子
- false [fɔls] *adj.* 虛偽的，假的

→ 請參看 9 ⑵₄ "Why is a false friend like the letter P?"

提起「影子 (shadow)」就會聯想到一段文章。請參見附錄 F

⑮ Q : Why does a person with his eyes closed resemble a bad school teacher?（為何一個閉上眼的人和一個差勁的學校老師相似？）

A : Because he keeps his pupils in darkness.

（因為他置他的學生於黑暗中／置瞳孔於黑暗之中。）

- pupil [`pjupl] *n.* 小學生；瞳孔

小學生稱為 pupil，中學生以上的學生都叫 student。大一學生為 freshman，俗稱新鮮人，因 "fresh" 即「新鮮的」。大二學生為 sophomore，大三學生為 junior，大四學生為 senior。研究生為 graduate student。注意發音：

- graduate [`grædʒuɪt] *adj.* 研究的
- graduate [`grædʒu,et] *v.* 畢業

同一個字，發音不同，意義就不一樣。

---

⑯ Q : Why does a man riding swiftly uphill resemble one who gives a young dog to his girl friend?

（為何一個騎馬快速上坡的人和一個把一隻小狗送給他女朋友的人相似？）

A : Because he gives a gallop up (gives a gal a pup).

（因為他策馬飛奔向上〔送一個女孩子一隻狗〕。）

→ "He gives a gallop up." (他飛奔向上。) 與 "He gives a gal a pup." (他給一個女孩一隻小狗。) 讀音很像。gal 加侖 gallon [`gælə] 的縮寫，亦作 "girl" 解。

- gallop [`gæləp] *n.* 疾馳，飛奔

- pup [pʌp] *n.* 小狗

17 Q：Why does an old man's head resemble a song sung by a very bad singer?（為何一個老人的頭和一首被爛歌手唱的歌相似？）

A：Because it is often terribly bawled (bald).

（因為它常被叫得很糟〔極度的禿頭〕。）

→ terribly bawled (狂吼亂叫) 與 terribly bald (極度的禿頭) 同音。

- bawl [bol] *n.* 叫罵聲 *v.* 大叫

- bald [bold] *adj.* 禿頭的

18 Q：Why does an oyster resemble a man of good sense?

（為何一個牡蠣和一位理性的人相似？）

A：Because it knows how to keep its mouth shut.（因為牠知道如何閉嘴。）

- keep one's mouth shut　閉嘴；不亂講話

例 Why don't you keep your mouth shut?（何不閉上你的狗嘴？）

19 Q：Why do good resolutions resemble ladies who faint in church?

（為何好的決心和暈倒在教堂的女士一樣？）

A：Because the sooner they are carried out the better.

（因為好的決心越快付諸實施越好／暈倒的女士越快抬出越好。）

- carry out　實行

提到 faint（昏倒）這個字，請參看 **Say when** 中第(51)題。

⑯ *Heads I Win*

硬幣 (coin) 的一面通常有偉人的人頭像，這面稱 **head**；反面則稱為 **tail**（尾巴）。玩遊戲時，常擲硬幣定勝負。有人比較滑頭，定下遊戲規則：「正面我贏，反面你輸。」(Head I win. Tail you lose.) 當然另一方絕對一直贏。

現在讓我們來看看有關 **Head** 的謎題：

1 Q: What is a head that glows?
（什麼頭會發光？）

A: headlight（前燈。）

→ 汽車車頭的燈稱為前燈，而非頭燈。

2 Q: What is a head that makes progress?（什麼頭會進步？）

A: Headway.（前進。）

3 Q: What is a head that pains?
（什麼頭會痛苦。）

A: Headache.（痛苦，頭痛。）

· toothache [`tuθ,ek] *n.* 牙痛

· stomachache [`stʌmək,ek] *n.* 腹痛

4 Q: What is a head that you see in newspapers?
（你在報上會看到什麼頭？）

A: Headlines.（頭條。）

5 Q: What is a head that chases people to do them no good?
（什麼頭追捕人而對人沒好處？）

A: Headhunter.（獵取人頭者。）

A headlight glows.

6. Q: What is a head that seats you in a hotel dining room?

（什麼頭能把你放置在旅社餐廳？）

A: Head waiter.（領班侍者。）

7. Q: What is a head that flows rapidly?（什麼頭能快速流動？）

A: headwaters.（水源。）

8. Q: What is a head that is the center of operations?（什麼頭是作戰中心？）

A: Headquarters.（總部。）

9. Q: What is a head that is bound to have its own way?

（什麼頭必須有自己的想法？）

A: Headstrong.（頑強。）

⑰ *Down the Garden Path*

　　這裡有若干有關蔬菜水果的謎題，大多採同音異義或同字異義的字，例如：pair，pear；leek，leak 等。

　　現在讓我們來看有關蔬菜水果的謎題：

① **Q**: What fruit is never found singly?（什麼水果絕不會單獨被找到？）

　　A: A pear (a pair).（梨子〔成對〕。）

→ pear 與 pair 同音。pear (pair) 成雙成對，當然單獨找不到。

> 梨與離同音，所以一對情侶是不能拿一個梨子來分著吃的，所以梨子不能分，否則就成了分梨（分離）了。有關梨的諧音字也有一句話：「蓮子心中苦，梨兒腹中酸」可解讀為：「憐子心中苦，離兒腹中酸。」
>
> → 蓮子的心味苦，而梨兒的心酸酸的。

② **Q**: What vegetable needs a plumber?（什麼蔬菜需要修水管工人？）

　　A: Leek (leak).（韭菜〔漏水〕。）

→ leak 與 leek 同音。

- leak [lik] *v.* 漏水
- leek [lik] *n.* 韭菜

例 The faucet is leaking.（水管正在漏水。）

> 將 leek 倒過來寫就成了 keel（龍骨）。

③ **Q**: What fruit is found on a penny?（什麼水果可在一分錢的硬幣上找到？）

　　A: Date.（棗子。）

→ date 亦作「日期」解。硬幣上鑄有日期。

④ **Q**: What vegetable has the most money in it?（什麼蔬菜有最多錢？）

　　A: Mint.（薄荷。）

→ mint 亦作「鑄幣廠」解。

5 **Q**: What vegetable do you find in crowded streetcars and bus?

（什麼蔬菜你可在擁擠的電車和公車上找到？）

A: Squash.（南瓜。）

→ squash 亦作「擁擠不堪的人群」。

6 **Q**: What vegetable is measured like diamonds?

（什麼蔬菜像鑽石一樣的單位？）

A: Carrots (carats).（胡蘿蔔〔克拉〕。）

→ carrots 與 carats 同音。鑽石 (diamond) 以克拉 (carats) 計。

carrot   *carot*

提起 diamond（鑽石），就會聯想到一首兒歌：「一閃一閃亮晶晶，…」

Twinkle, twinkle, little star;

How I wonder what you are,

Up above the world so high.

Like a diamond in the sky....

請參看附錄 I

---

7 **Q**: What vegetable hurts when you step on it?

（什麼蔬菜當你踩到時它會痛？）

A: Corn.（玉米／雞眼。）

→ corn 亦作「雞眼」解，你踩到雞眼當然會痛。

8 Q : What vegetable makes up the alphabet?（什麼蔬菜組成英文字母組？）

A : Lettuce (letters).（萵苣〔字母〕。）

> 有關 lettuce 的謎題可參看 4 (7) "What salad is best for newly weds?" 謎底是
>
> "Lettuce alone." (Let us alone!)
>
> → lettuce [ˋlɛtɪs] (萵苣) 與 letters [ˋlɛtɚz] (字母) 讀音極相近。

9 Q : What fruit will shock you when you touch it?

（當你摸到什麼水果時會觸電？）

A : Currant (current).（無核葡萄乾〔電流〕。）

→ 一般的葡萄乾稱為 raisin。currant 與 current 同音。

18 *What's the Good Word?*

國字謎題常常是「猜一字」，例如：「我的耳朵長，我姓王，今年十四歲，一心想進學堂。」謎底是「聽」。將謎題中的「耳」、「王」、「十四」和「一心」組合起來就成了「聽」。在英文謎語中，也有類似這種字，將不同的單字組合成一個字，例如："heart"（心臟）一字中就有 hear、he、ear。

現在讓我們來看看相關的謎題：

① Q: Is there a word in the English language that contains all the vowels?（英文語文中有否一個單字裡包括全部母音？）

A: Unquestionably.（無疑的。）

→ 從該字中可找到 a, e, i, o, u 五個母音。

② Q: What word of five letters has six left after you take two away?

（五個字母的單字，拿走兩個字母之後，剩下六個，是什麼字？）

A: Sixty.（六十。）

→ 將 sixty 中的兩個字母 ty 去掉，即得 six（六）。

③ Q: What word of ten letters might be spelled with five?

（什麼十個字母的字可用五個字母拼音？）

A: Expediency (XPDNC).（便利，權宜作法。）

→ 將 XPDNC 唸出來就是 expediency [ɪk`spidɪənsɪ]。

④ Q: Which word in the English language contains the greatest number of letters?（英文單字中那一個包含的字母最多？）

A: Antidisestablishmentarianism.（反上流社會主義。）

共有 28 個字母。此字的字根是 establish，作「設立」、「建立」解。establishment 變成名詞，disestablishment 為「不設立」或「不建立」，anti 加到前面有「反」的涵義，後面加 arianism，變為「主義」。這字幾乎在日常生活中看不到，只供文字遊戲罷了。

5 **Q**: What word of four syllables represents sin riding on a little animal?

（什麼四音節的單字代表罪惡騎在小動物上？）

A: Synonymous (Sin on a mouse).（同義的〔罪惡騎在老鼠上〕。）

→ synonymous 的發音與 sin on a mouse 很接近。

· **synonymous** [sɪˋnɑnəməs] *adj.* 同義的

· **synonym** [ˋsɪnəˌnɪm] *n.* 同義詞，近義詞

例 "Sad" and "unhappy" are synonyms.（「難過」和「不開心」是同義詞。）

6 **Q**: What word of eight letters is there from which you can subtract five and leave ten?（一個單字裡有八個字母，從其中減五個剩下十，是什麼字？）

A: Tendency.（傾向。）

→ 把 tendency 中五個字 dency 取出，只剩下 ten (十個)。

7 **Q**: In what common word does the letter O sound like the letter I?

（在那一個普通的單字中，字母 O 發 I 的音？）

A: Women.（女人）

→ 其中的 O 發 I 音。[ˋwɪmən] 女人，女人們

8 **Q**: Can you name two words that begin with P, in which the P is silent?（能否舉出兩個字的開頭都是 P，但 P 不發音？）

A: Psalms; pneumonia.（讚美詞；肺炎。）

→ psalm [sɑm] 讚美詞。字中連 "l" 也不發音。

· **pneumonia** [njuˋmonjə] *n.* 肺炎

例 You will catch pneumonia if you go out in the snow without a coat.

（如果你在下雪時出去不穿外套，你會得肺炎的。）

最常被引用的詩篇是 Psalms 23：

"The Lord is my shepherd. I have every think I need. He leads to fields of green grass and lets me rest in quiet pools of fresh water...."

---

9 **Q**: Can you name three common words, each containing a B, in which the B is silent?

（能否舉出三個普通的單字，每個單字都有一個 B 字母，其中 B 不發音？）

A : Doubt, debt and subtle.（懷疑，債務和微妙的。）

· doubt [daut] *n.* 懷疑

· debt [dɛt] *n.* 賭博

· subtle [`sʌtl̩] *adj.* 微妙的

以上三個字有 b，但不發音。另有 comb [kom]（梳子或梳頭髮）bomb [bɑm]（炸彈）
亦然。例：I comb my hair.（我梳我的頭髮。）
The bomb will soon explode.（這炸彈將立刻爆炸。）

⑩ **Q** : Can you name a word containing the letter l, in which the l is silent?（能否舉出一個單字其中包含字母 l，其中 l 不發音？）

A : Plaid.（蘇格蘭呢／彩格呢。）

· plaid [plæd] *n.* 蘇格蘭呢，彩格呢

⑪ **Q** : What word, by changing the position of one letter, becomes its opposite?（把什麼單字中的一個字母改換位置，其意義正好相反？）

A : United → Untied.（結合在一起 → 解除…的束縛。）

→ 將 united 中 i 和 t 互換位置即成 untied。

提到 united 一字，就會聯想到美國已故總統甘迺迪就職演説中的名言：
"United, there is little we cannot do.... Divided, there is little we can do...."
（若團結在一起，有很少的事我們做不到…。若彼此分散，我們能做的事很少…。）

⑫ **Q** : What word is it from which the whole may be taken and yet some will be left?（什麼字把它全部拿掉，仍然還剩一些？）

A : Wholesome.（健全的。）

→ 將 wholesome 中的 whole 拿掉，仍剩 some。

⑬ **Q** : What word of five letters has only one left when two letters are subtracted from it?

（五個字母的單字從中減去兩個字母還剩下一個，是什麼字？）

A : Stone.（石頭。）

→ 將 stone 中兩個字母 st 減去，剩下 one。

⑭ **Q** : What word, when deprived of one of its letters, makes you sick?

（什麼字，當其中一個字母去除，會使你生病？）

A : Music.（音樂。）

→ 將 music 中之 m 去掉，即成 usic，可唸成 you sick (你病了)。

⑮ **Q** : What word of fifteen letters is there from which you can subtract twelve and leave ten?

（什麼字有十五個字母，減去十二個字母後還剩十個？）

A : Pretentiousness.（狂妄。）

→ 將這個字十二個字母 pre tiousness 減去，剩下 ten (十)。

· pretentiousness [prɪˋtɛnʃəsnɪs] *n.* 狂妄

· pretentious [prɪˋtɛnʃəs] *adj.* 狂妄的

⑯ **Q** : Can you think of two eight-letter words, one of which has one syllable and the other five syllables?（你能否想出兩個皆有八個字母的字，其中之一有一個音節，另一個單字有五個音節？）

A : Strength and ideality.（堅強和理想境界。）

→ 前者只有一個音節，後者五個。

· strength [strɛŋkθ] *n.* 堅強

· ideality [ˏaɪdɪˋælɪtɪ] *n.* 理想境界

我們看字的變化：

· idea [aɪˋdiə] *n.* 計畫

· ideal [aɪˋdɪəl] *n.* 理想

· idealism [aɪˋdɪəlˏɪzəm] *n.* 理想主義

· idealist [aɪˋdɪəlɪst] *n.* 理想主義者

· idealize [aɪˋdɪəlˌaɪz] v. 把…理想化

(17) Q : What word of five syllables is it that if you take away one syllable, no syllable remains?

（什麼單字有五個音節，拿掉一個音節，則一個音節不剩？）

A : Monosyllable.（單音節。）

→ 將 monosyllable 中的 mo 去掉，剩下 no syllable (沒音節)。

(18) Q : What words can be pronounced quicker and shorter by adding another syllable to them?

（哪些字加了另一個音節給它們之後發音變得更快且更短？）

A : The words "quick" and "short."（「快」和「短」二字。）

→ 當 quick 和 short 各加一個音節 (er) 之後，就變成 "quicker" 且 "shorter"。

(19) Q : What is the longest word in the English language?

（英文裡最長的一個字是什麼？）

A : Smiles, because there is a mile between its first and last letter.

（微笑，因為第一到最後一個字母間有一哩長。）

→ 1 哩 (mile) = 1.6 公里 (kilometer)

Smiles, because there is a mile between the first and last letter.

⑲ *Turn-Around Riddles*

　　英文字是由字母拼成的，一個字順讀成字，但反讀不一定成字。這裡有一些英文字，反讀也是一個字，例如：leek（韭菜），反讀成 keel（龍骨）；mad（瘋狂）反讀成 dam（水壩）。

　　現在讓我們來看看以下的謎題：

① **Q**：Can you turn around a portion and get a snare?

　　（你能把「部分」轉過來變成「陷阱」嗎？）

A：Part → Trap.（部分 → 陷阱。）

→ 將 part 反轉過來即成 trap。

② **Q**：Can you turn around a short sleep and get a kitchen utensil?

　　（你能將「小睡」轉過來變成一件廚房「器皿」嗎？）

A：Nap → Pan.（小睡 → 平底鍋。）

③ **Q**：Can you turn around a well-known kind of cheese and get a word meaning "fabricated"?

　　（你能將有名的「起司」轉過來變成一個表示「製造」的字嗎？）

A：Edam → Made.（伊甸乾酪 → 製造。）

④ **Q**：Can you turn around a part of a ship and get a vegetable?

　　（你能把「船的一部分」轉過來變成一種「蔬菜」嗎？）

A：Keel → Leek.（龍骨 → 韭菜。）

⑤ **Q**：Can you turn around a part of a fence and get a prevaricator?

　　（你能把「籬笆的一部分」轉過來變成「推諉塞責的人」嗎？）

A：Rail → Liar.（欄杆 → 騙子。）

⑥ **Q**：Can you turn around a small one-masted sailboat and get little lakes?（你能把一艘「單桅的小帆船」轉過來變成「小湖」嗎？）

A : Sloop → Pools.（單桅小帆船 → 池，潭。）

⑦ Q : Can you turn around clever and get English trolley cars?

（你能將「聰明的」轉過來變成「英式電車」嗎？）

A : Smart → Trams.（聰敏的 → 電車。）

⑧ Q : Can you turn around wicked and get wide-awake?

（你能把「壞的」轉過來變成「完全清醒」嗎？）

A : Evil → Live.（邪惡 → 活潑的。）

> 電視上轉播球賽，若出現 "live [laɪv]" 字樣，表示是現場轉播，不是錄影紀錄片。

⑨ Q : Can you turn around a mouthful and get a stopper?

（你能將「滿口」轉過來變成「填塞物」嗎？）

A : Gulp → Plug.（狼吞虎嚥 → 塞子。）

⑩ Q : Can you turn around a strong, sharp taste and get an insect?

（你能將「強烈而辛辣的口味」轉過來變成「昆蟲」嗎？）

A : Tang → Gnat.（強烈的氣味 → 蚋蟲。）

⑪ Q : Can you read a sentence backward with exactly the same meaning as it is read forward?

（你能否倒著讀一個句子跟順著讀的意思完全一樣？）

A : You can cage a swallow, can't you, but you can't swallow a cage, can you?（你能將燕子關進鳥籠，不是嗎，但你不能嚥下一個鳥籠，是嗎？）

→ 將上句英文順讀或反過來讀都是一樣的。

> 中文句子也有精彩的一面，請看以下的句子：
> 「處處飛花飛處處，潺潺碧水碧潺潺。樹中雲連雲中樹，山外樓遮樓外山。」將這四句每一句反過來唸跟原文都是一樣的。中文裡還有很多迴文句也很美妙。寫在圓四周的五個字，從任何一個字開始順時針讀都成句。請看圖中五個字，可讀成五句：「心也可以清；也可以清心；可以清心也；以清心也可；清心也可以」。

還有更精彩的迴文句,將廿個字排成一圈。如圖:

→ 從任何一個字開始順時針讀都可成五言絕句,可得廿首詩。更妙的是從任一字開始反
時針讀亦成五言絕句,也可得廿首。總共可得四十首詩!

例如從「落」開始順時針讀:

「落雪飛芳樹,幽紅雨淡霞。薄月迷香霧,流風舞艷花。」

從「雪」開始順時針讀:

「雪飛芳樹幽,紅雨淡霞薄。月迷香霧流,風舞艷花落。」

仔細探討這廿個字是怎麼排出來的,似乎可以找出一點訣竅。在圓周上隔 180° 相對
的字幾乎都押韻,例如:「落,薄」,「幽,流」,「雪,月」,「芳,香」,「樹,霧」,「紅,
風」,「雨,舞」,「霞,花」。「飛」和「迷」用國語唸不押韻,但用臺語唸就押韻了,
「淡」與「艷」亦然。要成為五言絕句,一定要廿個字,如何在成千上萬個國字中找
出適當的廿個字來,很巧妙的排成圓圈圈,不是一件容易的工作,堪稱「文字排列組
合工程」(Word Combination and Permutation Engineering),當然這只是談笑,

或亦可稱之為另類藝術吧。愛因斯坦 (Einstein) 曾說過一句名言：

"Logic will get you from A to B. Imagination will take you everywhere."

（邏輯會把你從 A 帶到 B。想像會把你帶到任何地方。）

數理是走邏輯的，有一定的公式、定理、定律、法則…，照著邏輯從某一定點出發，遲早一定可以達到另一個預定的點。但文學、藝術就不一樣了，當然一些基本的邏輯規範需要遵守，但最重要的是要有開朗宏觀的想像力 (imagination)。寫一篇萬言的文章不難，但要寫一首能流傳千古的詩詞就不容易了。那排成圓圈的廿個字是妙絕傑作。

12 Q : Can you turn around fate and get a state of mind?

（你能將「命運」轉過來變成一種「心情的狀態」嗎？）

A : Doom → Mood. （命運 → 心情。）

(20) *Watch Your Step*

字譯 "Watch your step." 為「注意步伐。」走路要小心，不要摔倒。這裡所列的謎題是與錶 (watch) 有關。例如："What is it that has a face, but no head; hands, but no feet; yet travels everywhere and is usually running?"（什麼東西有面無頭；有手沒腳；能到處遊走，又經常在走？）謎底就是「錶」。錶有錶面 (face)，無頭 (head)；有手（hand，秒針，分針，時針）無腳；跟人到處遊走；而它也一直在走。

現在讓我們來看看有關 **Watch** 的謎題：

1 Q: What part of a watch supports a flower?（錶的什麼部分支持花朵？）

A: Stem.（莖／錶軸。）

2 Q: What part of a watch was used before by somebody else?

（錶的什麼部分被人用過？）

A: Second hand.（秒針。）

→ second hand 亦作「二手貨」解。

second hand

> 錶另有分針 (minute hand) 及時針 (hour hand)。

3 Q : What does a watch mark that is read by the secretary at a meeting?（錶上什麼標記是祕書在會議中要宣讀的？）

A : Minutes.（分／會議記錄。）

- minute [`mɪnɪt] *n.* 分（鐘）
- minute [mə`njut] 或 [maɪ`njut] *adj.* 極小的
- minute [`mɪnɪt] *n.* 會議記錄，議事錄

例 Before the committee started its work, the minutes of the last meeting were read out.（在委員會開始工作之前，上次會議記錄就先宣讀了。）

4 Q : What part of a watch is what the palmist studies?

（錶的什麼部分是看手相的人所要研究的？）

A : Hands. (hour hand, minute hand, second hand)

（手〔時針，分針，秒針〕。）

5 Q : What part of a watch do we use when we greet someone?

（錶的什麼部分是我們迎接人時要用的？）

A : Hour hand.（時針／我們的手。）

→ hour hand 與 our hand 同音。

6 Q : What part of a watch do women love to ornament?

（錶的什麼部分女人喜愛做裝飾品？）

A : Jewels.（寶石。）

7 Q : What part of a watch will always give you a cool drink?

（錶的什麼部分總是供應你冷飲？）

A : Spring.（發條／泉水。）

→ 機械式的錶須上發條。

8 Q : Why is a watch like a river?（為何錶像河流？）

A : Because it won't run long without winding.

（因為錶不上發條就走不久／河流不蜿蜒則流不遠。）

9 Q: Why should a man always sear a watch when he travels in a desert?（人在沙漠旅行時，為何總是將錶吸乾？）

A: Because every watch has a spring in it.（因為每隻錶內都有發條。）

→ spring 亦作「甘泉」解。

· sear [sɪr] *v.* 使乾枯

10 Q: Why are the hours from one to twelve like good policemen?

（為何從一點到十二點的時間像個好警察？）

A: Because they are always on the watch.（因為他們總是在錶上／值勤。）

· **on the watch** 在錶上；值班

21 Kate's a Good Skate

　　kate 無意義，也就是字典裡沒有 kate 這個單字，但前面加一個 s 成 skate 就是溜冰鞋。字尾為 cate 之字，其 cate 之發音與 kate 相同，例如：educate [ˈɛdʒə,ket]（教育），locate [loˈket]（定位），以下有若干謎題，其謎底之字尾皆為 cate。

　　現在讓我們來看看有關 cate 的謎題：

1 Q: What kate likes school?（什麼 kate 喜歡學校？）

　A: Educate.（教育。）

2 Q: What kate makes things invisible?（什麼 kate 使東西看不見？）

　A: Eradicate.（消滅。）

　・ eradicate [ɪˈrædɪ,ket] *v.* 消滅

　・ to eradicate poverty/ crime/ disease　消滅貧窮／犯罪／疾病

> 美國已故總統迺迪就職演說中的名言：
>
> "Together let us explore the stars, conquer the deserts, eradicate disease, tap the ocean depths and encourage the arts and commerce."（讓我們同心協力探索星星，征服沙漠，消滅疾病，推敲海洋的深處，並且鼓勵藝術和交流。）

3 Q: What kate is twin?（什麼 kate 是雙胞胎？）

　A: Duplicate.（複製。）

4 Q: What kate is always showing the way?（什麼 kate 經常指引方向？）

　A: Indicate.（指示。）

5 Q: What kate finds things for you?（什麼 kate 為你找到東西？）

　A: Locate.（定位。）

6 Q: What kate can't breathe?（什麼 kate 不能呼吸？）

　A: Suffocate.（窒息。）

　・ suffocate [ˈsʌfə,ket] *v.* 窒息

例 The baby suffocated under its pillow.（嬰兒壓在枕頭下窒息而死。）

> 另有一個字 smother [`smʌðɚ] 亦作「使窒息」解。讀者可參看 Bible 中「所羅門王的智慧」(*The Wisdom of King Solomon*)。

commumicate

7 Q : What kate talks and writes a lot?

（什麼 kate 談話和寫字都多？）

A : Communicate.（通訊。）

8 Q : What kate is in many newspapers?

（什麼 kate 在很多報紙上？）

A : Syndicate.（商業團體。）

· syndicate [`sɪndɪket] *v.* 組成辛迪加

· syndicate [`sɪndɪkɪt] *n.* 商業團體

9 Q : What kate is full of advice?

（什麼 kate 充滿忠告？）

A : Advocate.（提倡者。）

· advocate [`ædvəkɪt] *n.* 提倡者

· advocate [`ædvə‚ket] *v.* 提倡

例 He advocates a reduction in tax.（他主張減稅。）

10 Q : What kate is good at getting out of tight places?

（什麼 kate 善於脫離困境？）

A : Extricate.（救生。）

· in a tight place　處於困境

例 He is in a tight place.（他身處困境。）

11 Q : What kate keeps the machinery going smoothly?

（什麼 kate 使機器運轉順暢？）

A : Lubricate.（潤滑。）

12 Q : What kate is inclined to be sick?（什麼 kate 傾向於病痛？）

A：Delicate.（柔弱的。）

- delicate [`dɛləkət] *adj.* 易碎的；嬌弱的
- be inclined to 有…之傾向

例 I am inclined to change my mind.（我有改變主意的傾向。）

⑬ **Q**：What kate is always chewing on something?

（什麼 kate 總是在嚼東西？）

A：Masticate.（咀嚼。）

- masticate [`mæstə,ket] *v.* 咀嚼

⑭ **Q**：What kate is clever at predicting things?（什麼 kate 精於預測事情？）

A：Prognosticate.（預言。）

- prognosticate [prag`nɑstɪ,ket] *v.* 預言
- be clever at 擅於

例 He is clever at solving difficult problems.（他善於解難題。）

⑮ **Q**：What kate consecrates things?（什麼 kate 奉獻東西？）

A：Dedicate.（奉獻。）

- dedicate [`dɛdə,ket] *v.* 奉獻

例 He dedicated his life to helping the poor.（他奉獻他的一生幫助窮困的人。）

I dedicated my first book to my wife.（我把第一部著作獻給我的妻子。）

⑯ **Q**：What kate gives up the throne?（什麼 kate 放棄王位？）

A：Abdicate.（退位。）

- abdicate [`æbdə,ket] *v.* 退位，讓位

例 The king abdicated the throne.（國王退位了。）

⑰ **Q**：What two kates tell fibs?（哪兩個 kate 撒小謊？）

A：Fabricate and prevaricate.（捏造和搪塞。）

- fabricate [`fæbrɪket] *v.* 編造

例 He fabricated the whole story.（他編造整個故事。）

· **prevaricate** [prɪ`værə,ket] *v.* 推諉，支吾，搪塞

· **fib** [fɪb] *n.* 撒小謊

· **to tell a fib** 撒小謊

例 What a fibber he is!（他是一個多麼愛撒小謊的人啊！）

⑱ Q: What kate is a good peacemaker?（什麼 kate 是好的和平使者？）

A: Placate.（和解。）

· **placate** [`pleket] *v.* 安撫，使息怒

例 I placated her by singing songs.（我用唱歌來安撫她。）

> 請留意：將 peacemaker 中的 e 去掉就變成 pacemaker（心律調節器）。

⑲ Q: What kate is always leaving places?（什麼 kate 總是離開許多地方？）

A: Vacate.（退出。）

· **vacate** [`veket] *v.* 使搬出

例 You must vacate your room by 5 o'clock.（你必須在五點前空出房間。）

⑳ Q: What kate justifies people?（什麼 kate 為人辯護？）

A: Vindicate.（辯明，辯護。）

· **vindicate** [`vɪndəket] *v.* 為…辯護

例 The report vindicates him.（這報告證明他是清白的。）

㉑ Q: What kate is always disapproving?（什麼 kate 總是不贊成？）

A: Deprecate.（反對。）

· **deprecate** [`dɛprə,ket] *v.* 不贊成；反對

例 I strongly deprecate the use of power.（我強烈反對使用權力。）

㉒ Q: What kate gets people in trouble?（什麼 kate 使人困擾？）

A: Implicate.（涉及。）

· **implicate** [`ɪmplɪ,ket] *v.* 涉及，表示（某人）與…有牽連（尤指犯罪）

例 The letter implicates him in the robbery.（這信表明他與搶劫案有牽連。）

22　*Riddles with the Dumb Endings*

　　Dumb，啞巴，啞的。有口不會言，謂之「啞」，有眼不能看，謂之「盲 (blind)」，有耳不能聽，謂之「聾 (deaf)」。有的單字之字尾為 dom，其發音與 dumb 相同。

　　現在我們來看看有多少字是以 dom 為字尾的：

① Q：What is dumb but knowing?（什麼是 dumb 但卻博學？）

A：Wisdom.（智慧。）

・knowledge [`nɑlɪʤ] *n.* 知識

・wisdom [`wɪzdəm] *n.* 智慧

→ know 加 edge（邊緣）就成了 knowledge（當然 know 與 edge 之間要置一個字母 l）或 know 加 ledge（壁架）也成了 knowledge。

Knowledge is knowing a fact.

知識與智慧的分際在哪裡？有一句話詮釋得很恰當：

Knowledge is knowing a fact. Wisdom is knowing what to do with that fact.

（知識是知道事實。智慧是知道用那樣事實做出什麼來。）

→ 知識由 know（知）而來；智慧由 wise（智）而來。

2 Q：What is dumb but liberty-loving?（什麼是 **dumb** 但卻是愛好自由的？）

A：Freedom.（自由。）

> 有句自由的名言：Without freedom, I would rather die.（無自由，毋寧死。）
>
> → freedom（自由）由 free（自由的）而來。

3 Q：What is dumb and also tiresome?（什麼是 **dumb** 卻也是令人厭煩的？）

A：Boredom.（厭煩。）

・bore [bor] *v.* 使厭煩

例 He bored me by talking for hours about his children.

（他大談他的小孩好幾個小時，使我厭煩。）

・boring [ˋborɪŋ] *adj.* 無聊的

例 The job is boring.（這工作枯燥乏味。）

・bored [bord] *adj.* 厭煩的

例 He is bored with the job.（他對這工作感到厭煩。）

・boredom [ˋbordəm] *n.* 厭煩

例 I don't want to conceal my boredom.（我不想掩飾我的厭倦。）

4 Q：What is dumb and infrequent?（什麼是 **dumb** 且稀有的？）

A：Seldom.（罕有的。）

→ frequent *adj.* 常常的，由 frequency（頻率）一字而來。

・infrequent [ɪnˋfrikwənt] *adj.* 不常的，稀有的

5 Q：What is dumb but full of high public officers?

（什麼是 **dumb** 但充滿了高級官員？）

A：Officialdom.（官場。）

→ office（辦公室），加 er 後變成 officer（官員），再將 office 加 holder 就變為
officeholder（政府官員，任公職者）。

> 提到這個字 **office holder** 就聯想起「禮運大同篇」裡的文句：
>
> 「大道之行也，天下為公。選賢與能，講信修睦…。」

"When the great way prevails, the world community is equally shared by all. The worthy and able are chosen as officeholders. Mutual confidence is fostered and good neighborliness cultivated...."

請參見附錄 G

6 **Q**: What is dumb but sacrifices itself for ideal?

（什麼是 dumb 但卻為理想而犧牲？）

A: Martyrdom.（殉道。）

‧ martyr [`mɑrtɚ] *n.* 殉道者

例 She enjoys being a martyr.（她享受苦行者的樂趣。）

‧ martyrdom [`mɑrtɚdəm] *n.* 殉難；殉教，殉道；受苦

7 **Q**: What is dumb and ruled by a powerful monarch?

（什麼是 dumb 而被一個有權力的國王統治？）

A: Kingdom.（王國。）

23 *Do You Know Your Aunts?*

以 ant（螞蟻）為字尾的字，其發音與 aunt（伯母）相同。我們可藉猜謎的時刻，每天都可記一些以 ant 為字尾的字。

現在讓我們來看看有多少字是以 ant 為字尾的：

1 Q : What aunt provides a place for you to eat?

（什麼 aunt 為你提供一個場所吃東西？）

A : Restaurant.（餐廳。）

→ 餐廳吃東西的地方，可得到舒解和休息，所以字首為 rest (休息)，很合邏輯。

· restaurant [`rɛstərənt] *n.* 餐廳，飯店

2 Q : What aunt is a sweet-smelling aunt?（什麼 aunt 是氣味芬芳的 aunt？）

A : Fragrant.（有香味的。）

· fragrant [`fregrənt] *adj.* 芬芳的

例 The air in the garden is fragrant.（花園裡的空氣芳香。）

· fragrance [`fregrəns] *n.* 芳香

3 Q : What aunt is a despotic aunt?（什麼 aunt 是專橫的 aunt？）

A : Tyrant.（暴君。）

· tyrant [`taɪrənt] *n.* 暴君

· tyranny [`tɪrənɪ] *n.* 暴政

· despot [`dɛspət] *n.* 專制統治者

· despotic [dɪ`spɑtɪk] *adj.* 專橫的

4 Q : What aunt is a vagabond aunt?

（什麼 aunt 是個無賴的 aunt？）

A : Vagrant.（無賴。）

· vagrant [`vegrənt] *n.* 流浪者，乞丐

· vagabond [`vægə͵bɑnd] *n.* 懶漢；流浪者

5 **Q** : What aunt is a schoolteacher aunt?（什麼 aunt 是學校教師 aunt？）

A : Pedant.（學究。）

· pedant [`pɛdn̩t] *n.* 學究，迂夫子

6 **Q** : What aunt is a hard, unyielding aunt?（什麼 aunt 是堅定不屈的 aunt？）

A : Adamant.（堅強不屈的。）

· adamant [`ædə͵mænt] *adj.* 堅定的

例 I am adamant that you should come.（我堅持要你們來。）

7 **Q** : What aunt is a zestful aunt?（什麼 aunt 是充滿趣味的 aunt？）

A : Piquant.（有趣的。）

· piquant [`pikənt] *adj.* 開心的，使人興奮的

例 It is a piquant situation.（那是使人得意揚揚的場面。）

· zest [zɛst] *n.* 風趣

· zestful [zɛstfəl] *adj.* 有趣味性的

8 **Q** : What aunt is a conspicuous aunt?（什麼 aunt 是著名的 aunt？）

A : Flagrant.（罪惡昭彰的。）

· flagrant [`flegrənt] *adj.* 明目張膽的，罪惡昭彰的

例 He is a flagrant liar.（他是個說謊不臉紅的人。）

請留意 flagrant 與 23 ⑵中的 fragrant（芬芳的）只是一字之差。
---

9 **Q** : What aunt is a dangerous aunt?（什麼 aunt 是危險的 aunt？）

A : Malignant.（有惡意的。）

· malignancy [mə`lıgnənsı] *n.* 惡毒

· malignant [mə`lıgnənt] *adj.* 惡毒的

· malignant tumour 惡性腫瘤

10 **Q** : What aunt is a bossy aunt?（什麼 aunt 是霸道的 aunt？）

A : Dominant.（有統治權的。）

· dominant [ˋdɑməˌnənt] *adj.* 佔優勢的，最顯著的

例 The right hand is dominant in most people. （大多數人的右手是優勢手。）

Pollution is the dominant theme of the conference.

（污染是大會首要的議題。）

⑪ Q : What aunt is a calculating aunt? （什麼 aunt 是計算的 aunt？）

A : Accountant. （會計師。）

· accountant [əˋkauntənt] *n.* 會計師

例 He is an accountant in our company. （他是我們公司的會計師。）

⑫ Q : What aunt is an uninformed aunt? （什麼 aunt 是無知的 aunt？）

A : Ignorant. （無知的。）

· ignorant [ˋɪgnərənt] *adj.* 無知的

· ignorance [ˋɪgnərəns] *n.* 無知

例 He is ignorant about computers. （他對電腦一竅不通。）

Ignorance of the law is no excuse. （對法律的無知不能成為藉口。）

⑬ Q : What aunt is a beggar aunt? （什麼 aunt 是乞丐 aunt？）

A : Mendicant. （乞丐。）

· mendicant [ˋmɛndɪkənt] *n.* 乞丐 *adj.* 以乞討為生的

例 He hates working. He would rather be a mendicant.

（他憎恨工作。他寧做一個以乞討為生的人。）

⑭ Q : What aunt is a prevailing aunt? （什麼 aunt 是佔優勢的 aunt？）

A : Predominant. （卓越的。）

· predominant [prɪˋdɑməˌnet] *adj.* 佔優勢的；支配性的

例 Bright blue is the predominant color in the room.

（寶藍色是這房間的主色。）

⑮ Q : What aunt is an inharmonious aunt? （什麼 aunt 是不調諧的 aunt？）

A : Discordant. （不調和的。）

・ discordant [dɪs`kɔrdn̩t] *adj.* 不一致的，不調和的

16 **Q** : What aunt is an impertinent aunt?（什麼 aunt 是鹵莽的 aunt？）

　　A : Flippant.（輕率的。）

　　・ flippant [`flɪpənt] *adj.* 輕率的

　　例 An office is scarcely the place for such flippant remarks on sex.
　　　（辦公室絕不是輕率談論性的地方。）

17 **Q** : What aunt makes good jelly?（什麼 aunt 可做出好的果醬？）

　　A : Currant.（無核小葡萄乾。）

　　・ currant [`kɝənt] *n.* 無核小葡萄乾

　　・ current [`kɝənt] *n.* 電流

> 請留意 currant（無核小葡萄乾）與 current（電流）只是一個字母之差！

18 **Q** : What aunt is like a still pond?（什麼 aunt 像平靜的池塘？）

　　A : Stagnant.（停滯的。）

　　・ stagnant [`stægnənt] *adj.* 不流動的，停滯的

　　例 The industrial output has remained stagnant.（工業生產已停滯不前。）

19 **Q** : What are the biggest kind of aunts?（什麼是最大的 aunt？）

　　A : Giants.（巨人。）

20 **Q** : What aunt is a traveling aunt?（什麼 aunt 是旅行的 aunt？）

　　A : Itinerant.（巡迴的。）

　　・ itinerant [aɪ`tɪnərənt] *adj.* 巡迴的，流動的

　　例 He is an itinerant preacher.（他是個巡迴的傳教士。）

24 *Riddle Me This*

　　"riddle" 一字為「謎」，亦可作「解謎」解。"Riddle me this!" 即「讓我來解此謎。」有若干謎題，頗費思索，不易猜透，及至揭開謎底，又令人驚嘆不已。在日常生活中，若能善用奇言妙語，當可使談話更為生動，使生活更富樂趣。昔日曾有人問美國已故總統林肯：「人的雙腿多長才最合適？」林肯想了一會兒，答：「長可及地最合適。」真是奇言妙語呀！

　　現在讓我們來看看相關的謎題：

1 Q：What amount of money can be divided fifty-fifty between two persons, giving one person a hundred times more than the other?

（把多少錢分給二人，各得五十對五十，而其中一人所得為另一人的一百倍？）

A：Fifty dollars and fifty cents.（五十元與五十分／五角。）

→ 一元等於十角，一角等於十分。此題的謎底為 50.5 元，一人分得 50 元，另一人得 0.5 元，50 為 0.5 的 100 倍。

2 Q：There is one thing that no one knows any more about no matter how much it is looked into. What is it?

（有一樣東西，無論怎麼往裡看，也不會對它知道的更多，那是什麼？）

A：A mirror.（一面鏡子。）

→ look into 作「調查」解。字譯：往裡看。

・**look into** 調查

例 I'll look into the matter.（我要調查此事。）

> 由於謎底是鏡子，所以用 "look into"（看進去）。對著鏡子往裡看，再怎麼看，鏡子仍是鏡子，也不會對它知道的更多。

3 Q：A man bought two fish and had three when he got home. How did this happen?（一個人買了兩條魚，回家後變成三條，是怎麼回事？）

A : He had two fish, and one smelt.

（他有兩條魚，和一條銀白魚／但一條發臭了。）

→ fish (魚)，單數和複數同形，smelt 為 smell 的過去分詞，作「發臭」解。smelt 亦作「銀白魚」解。

・ smelt [smɛlt] *v.* (smell/ smelt/ smelt) 聞

④ Q : On which side of a church does a yew tree grow?

（水松樹長在教堂的那一邊？）

A : On the outside. （外邊。）

→ 謎底不是 left side 或 right side，而是 outside。

⑤ Q : The first part of an odd number is removed and it becomes even. What number is it?（把一個奇數的第一部分拿走就變成了偶數，是什麼數？）

A : Seven. （七。）

→ seven (7) 是奇數，把 seven 的第一部分 (字母 s) 拿走，就變成了 even (偶數)。

在數學中，個位數為奇數 (1, 3, 5, 7, 9) 的任意數皆為奇數 (odd)。

→ 例如 963352639 為奇數，將第一部分 (即前面第一位數 9) 拿走，變為 63352639 仍為奇數。謎題是在玩文字遊戲，seven 去首變為 even。提到去首就聯想起一則謎語：「什麼動物去首後變成另一種動物？」謎底是 "fox" (狐狸)，因去首後變成 "ox" (公牛)。此謎題在本書中可找到。

⑥ Q : At what time of life does everyone weigh the most?

（人在一生中何時最重？）

A : When he is the heaviest. （當他最重的時候。）

當然 "When he is the heaviest, he weighs the most." 這類謎題的謎底是用謎題的另一說法作答，可說是同義異句法。

⑦ Q : What two vegetables begin and end with the same two letters in the same order?

（那兩種蔬菜的開頭和末尾兩個字母相同且其排列次序亦同？）

A : Tomato and onion.（番茄和洋蔥。）

→ tomato 前後二字母皆為 "to"。onion 前後二字母皆為 "on"。

> 提到這兩個字，就聯想到「那兩個字前後二字母對稱？」謎底是 "radar and level"（雷達和水平）。radar 前後二字母對稱，level 亦然。

8 Q : Can you name eight different subjects taught in school or college that end in ics?（能否列舉學校或學院所開授的八門課，其字尾皆為 ics？）

A : Economics, ethics, mathematics, physics, mechanics, dramatics, civics, and calisthenics.

（經濟學，倫理學，數學，物理學，機械學，戲劇學，公民學和柔軟體操。）

9 Q : Soldiers mark time with their feet, what does the same thing with the hands?（士兵用腳標示時間，什麼東西用手做同樣的事？）

A : Watch.（錶。）

→ 因錶有 hour hand (時針)、minute hand (分針) 和 second hand (秒針)，錶用這些手 (針) 標示時間。題中 "mark time" 亦可作「士兵踏步，打拍子」解，故謎題可解為「士兵用腳踏步。」

10 Q : Sisters and brothers have I none, but that man's father is my father's son. Who am I looking at?

（我無兄弟亦無姊妹，不過那人的父親是我父親的兒子，我在看的是誰？）

A : My own son.（我自己的兒子。）

> 請讀者自己檢視一下，是否正確。

11 Q : Suppose there was a cat in each corner of the room, a cat sitting opposite each cat; a cat looking at each cat; and a cat sitting on each cat's tail. How many cats would there be?

（房間裡每個角落有一隻貓，每隻貓面對每一隻貓坐著；每隻貓看著每一隻貓；每隻貓坐在每一隻貓的尾巴上。究竟有幾隻貓？）

A : Four. Each cat was sitting on its own tail.

（四隻。每隻貓都坐在牠自己的尾巴上。）

⑫ **Q** : A girl had an aunt who was in love. She sent her an animal whose name urged the aunt to run away and get married. The aunt sent her back a fruit that brought the message that this was impossible. What was the animal and what was the fruit?

（一個女孩有一位在戀愛中的姑姑，她送給她一隻動物，牠的名字鼓勵她姑姑逃走與人結婚。她姑姑回送她一種水果，這水果的名字傳達一種信息表示那是不可能的。究竟是什麼動物和水果？）

A : Antelope (aunt, elope) and cantaloupe (can't elope).

（羚羊〔姑姑，私奔〕和羅馬甜瓜〔不能私奔〕。）

→ antelope [`æntlˌop] *n.* 羚羊。發音與 "aunt elope" 相近。cantaloupe 發音與 "can't elope" 相近。

・ elope [ɪ`lop] *v.* 私奔

⑬ **Q** : What are two of the greatest modern miracles?

（近代兩件最大的奇蹟是什麼？）

A : The deaf mute who picked up a wheel and spoke, and the blind man who picked up a hammer and saw.

（耳聾的啞巴拾起車輪就說話，瞎子撿起鐵鎚就看得見。）

→ 當然這是大奇蹟。但是題中的 spoke 是 speak (說) 的過去式，亦作「車輪的輻」解。saw 是 see (看) 的過去式，亦作「鋸子」或「鋸東西」解。謎題的字譯為「啞巴拾起車輪和車輻，而瞎子拾起鐵鎚和鋸子。」

⑭ **Q** : A duck, a frog and a skunk went to the circus. Each had to have a dollar to get in. Which got in, and which didn't?（一隻鴨，一隻青蛙和一隻臭鼬去看馬戲團。每個都得有一塊錢才能入場。誰能進場，誰不能？）

A : The duck got in because she had a bill.

（鴨子能進場，因為牠有一張支票／一張嘴。）

The frog got in on his green-back.

（青蛙能進場，因為牠有綠背紙幣／綠色的背。）

But the poor old skunk couldn't get in because he had only a cent (scent) and it was a bad one. （但是可憐的老臭鼬不能進場，因為牠只有一分錢〔臭味〕，而這一分錢〔臭味〕是很糟的一種。）

- bill [bɪl] *n.* 紙幣，鈔票
- greenback [`grin͵bæk] *n.* 美鈔
- scent [sɛnt] *n.* 臭氣
- skunk [skʌŋk] *n.* 臭鼬

⑮ Q：Abraham Lincoln was asked how long a man's legs should be to be the most serviceable. What was his answer?

（林肯被問到人的雙腿該多長才最為合用。他的回答是什麼？）

A：Long enough to reach the ground. （長可及地。）

→ 無論腿長或腿短，只要能雙腳及於地就最合用，真是奇言妙語呀。

⑯ Q：The king's fool offended him and was condemned to death. The king said, "You have been a good fool, so I will let you choose the manner of your death." What manner of death did the fool choose? （一個笨蛋冒犯了國王而被判死刑。國王說：「你一向是個好笨蛋，所以我讓你自己選擇你死的方式。」這個笨蛋選擇什麼死法？）

A：The death of old age. （壽終正寢。）

→ 這又是奇言妙語！這笨蛋事實上一點都不笨，他不選打死，吊死，溺死…的死法，選擇最自然的死法「壽終正寢」。這題令人聯想起一則類似的笑話：一個生前既吝嗇 (stingy) 又貪婪 (greedy) 的守財奴，死後到地府報到。閻羅王問他：「你生前貪財怕死，一毛不拔，我令你投胎為狗，不過你可選擇變公狗或母狗。」此人答道：「小的願為母狗。」閻王驚問：「當母狗要生小狗，比較辛苦，為何

想當？」此人答道：「因為臨財母狗 (母苟) 得，臨難母狗 (母苟) 免。」亦奇言妙語也！

17 Q: How many eggs can a man eat on an empty stomach?

（一個人空著肚子時能吃多少蛋？）

A: None. As soon as he begins to eat even one bite of an egg, his stomach is no longer empty.

（一個都沒有。他一旦開始吃就算只吃了一小口蛋，他的胃就不再是空的了。）

18 Q: An old woman in a red cloak was crossing a field in which there was a goat. What strange transformations suddenly took place?

（一個著紅斗篷的老婦人穿過田野，田野上有隻山羊。有什麼樣的奇妙轉變會突然發生？）

A: The goat turned to butter (butt her) and the old woman became a scarlet runner.（山羊變成了牛油〔用羊角撞她〕而老婦人變成了鮮紅色的滑板／穿紅衣的賽跑選手。）

→ 句中 butter (牛油) 與 butt her (撞她) 同音。

‧ cloak [klok] *n.* 斗篷，披風

‧ scarlet [`skɑrlɪt] *adj.* 鮮紅色的

‧ runner [`rʌnɚ] *n.* 賽跑選手，滑板

‧ butt [bʌt] *n.* 撞 *v.* (用頭或角) 撞，頂，牴

例 The goat gave me a butt in the stomach.（山羊撞了我的肚子。）

19 Q: Can you spell "blind pig" with two letters?

（你能用兩個字母拼出「瞎眼的豬」嗎？）

A: Pg (pig without an eye).（**pg**〔pig 沒有 i〕。）

→ i 與 eye 同音，沒有 i (eye) 的 pig (即 pg) 當然是瞎眼的。

20 Q: One boy calls his girlfriend "postscript." What do you think her real name is?（一個男孩叫他的女朋友為 "再者"，你認為她真正的名字是什麼？）

A : Adeline Moore (Add a line more).（愛德蘭茉爾〔附加一行〕。）

→ Adeline Moore 與 Add a line more 二者讀音相近。

21 Q : Why is a barefoot boy like an Alaskan Eskimo?

（為何一個赤腳的男孩子像阿拉斯加的愛斯基摩人？）

A : Because he wears no shoes (wears snow shoes).

（因為他沒穿鞋〔穿雪鞋〕。）

→ wears no shoes (沒穿鞋) 與 wears snow shoes (穿雪鞋) 二者讀音同。

> 提到 shoes 就聯想到一句名言：
>
> I had no shoes and complained until I met a man who had no feet.
>
> （我沒鞋穿而抱怨直到我遇到一個人他沒有雙腳。）

22 Q : What is the happiest state?（那一州最快樂？）

A : Maryland (Merryland).（馬利蘭州〔快樂地〕。）

· merry [ˋmɛrɪ] *adj.* 快樂的

· marry [ˋmærɪ] *v.*（與…）結婚，娶，嫁

> 看到 merry 這個字，就會聯想到 marry（結婚）。這兩個字只是一個字母之差，結了婚就會快樂。依 a、e、i、o、u 母音的次序，先 a 後 e，所以 marry 先，才 merry 後。臺語娶老婆叫「娶某」（以台語發音），但臺語的「娶某」跟英文的 "trouble" 發音相近，所以有句好玩的說法：「你若『娶某』，你就會有 "trouble"。」

23 Q : What part of London is in France?（倫敦的那一部分在法國？）

A : The letter N.（字母 N。）

→ London 一字中的字母 n 也在 France 中。

24 Q : What continent do you see when you look in the mirror in the morning?（你早晨照鏡子時，會看到那一洲？）

A : You see Europe (you're up).（你看到歐洲〔你起來了〕。）

→ "You see Europe." 與 "You see you're up." 發音相近。

· Europe [ˋjurəp] *n.* 歐洲

㉕ Q : Why is the Mississippi the most talkative of rivers?

（為何密西西比河是最多話的河？）

A : Because it has a dozen mouths.

（因為它有一打嘴巴／因為它有十二個出口。）

㉖ Q : Which of the West Indian island does a maker of preserved fruits resemble?（西印度群島中那一個島和醃漬水果的製造者相似？）

A : Jamaica (jam-maker).（牙買加島〔果醬製造者〕。）

→ Jamaica 與 jam-maker 二者發音相近。

㉗ Q : What is it that is found in the very center of America and Australia?

（在美國和澳洲的正中央被找到的是什麼？）

A : The letter R.（字母 R。）

→ 因為在 America 一字的正中央是字母 R，Australia 亦然。句中的 "very" 不可譯成「非常」或「很」，在這裡它表示「正是」，例如：This is the very book that I want. (我想要的「正是」這本書。）

㉘ Q : Why is the leaning tower of Pisa like Greenland?

（為何比薩斜塔像格林蘭？）

A : Because it is oblique (so bleak).（因為它是斜的〔如此淒涼〕。）

→ "It is oblique."（它是斜的。）與 "It is so bleak."（這裡如此淒涼。）發音相近。

· oblique [əˋblik] adj. 傾斜的

· bleak [blik] adj. 淒涼的

㉙ Q : If Ireland should sink, what would float?

（假設愛爾蘭沉了，什麼會浮起來？）

A : Cork.（柯克城／軟木。）

→ 這謎題是假設語氣，所以用 "should"，"would" 過去式的形式。

㉚ Q : What sea would you like to be in on a wet, rainy day?

（在潮溼而多雨的一天裡，你喜歡在什麼海中？）

A : Adriatic (a dry attic). (義大利東岸的亞得里亞海〔一間乾燥的閣樓〕。)

→ Adriatic 與 "a dry attic" 音相近。

· attic [`ætɪk] *n.* 閣樓，頂樓

記得早年在美國印第安那 (Indiana) 州西拉法葉 (West Lafayette) 鎮的 Purdue 大學唸書時，為了省錢住在居民家的閣樓上。那時一般住房月租要卅五美元，我住閣樓只要十八美元。床舖就在斜斜的屋頂下，有時清晨被鬧鐘叫醒，突然坐起時，還會撞到頭哩！

25 *For Bigger, Better or Worse*

　　形容詞有三級：原級、比較級和最高級。例如：big → bigger → biggest；good → better → best；bad → worse → worst。提到 "bigger" 這個字就聯想起一則笑話。一位生意人認識一個美國朋友。幾年後又到他家作客，看到老美的女兒多年不見長大了，於是用臺語式的英文說："Your daughter is bigger and bigger."（你女兒的肚子越來越大。）老美聽完後氣炸了。正確的說法是："She is really growing."

　　現在讓我們來看看有關 Bigger 的謎語：

1　Q：A man named Bigger got married. How did he compare in size with his wife?（一個人名叫 Bigger 結婚了。他和他太太在個子大小上如何比較？）

　　A：He was larger, for he always had been Bigger.

　　（他比較大些，因為他一直是比較大些／一直是 Bigger 先生。）

2　Q：Mrs. Bigger had a baby. Now who was bigger?

　　（Bigger 太太有一個嬰兒。現在誰比較大？）

　　A：The baby, because he was a little Bigger.

　　（嬰兒比較大，因為他 a little Bigger。）

　　→ a little bigger，表示「稍大一點」。

3　Q：Mr. Bigger dies. Then who was bigger?

　　（Bigger 先生死了。然後誰比較大？）

　　A：Mrs. Bigger, for she was Bigger still.

　　（Bigger 太太比較大，因為她仍然是 Bigger 太太。）

　　→ bigger still 表示「仍然比較大」。

4　Q：What is better than presence of mind in a railroad accident?

　　（當火車發生意外時，有什麼比「心在」更好？）

　　A：Absence of body.（身不在。）

→ 在意外中，當然「身不在」比「心在」好。

· presence [`prɛzn̩s] *n.* 出席

· absence [`æbsn̩s] *n.* 缺席

· presence of body　字譯：身體出席。意即「身在」。

· absence of body　字譯：身體缺席。意即「身不在」。

用同樣的架構，我們可寫出：

presence of mind　心在

absence of mind　心不在

例：Don't be presence of body but absence of mind.

　　Don't be present in body but absent in mind.（不要人在心不在。）

　　Be presence of body and presence of mind.

　　Be present in body and present in mind.（要人在心在。）

---

⑤ Q：What is worse than a giraffe with a sore throat?

　　（什麼比長頸鹿喉嚨痛更糟？）

A：A centipede with sore feet.（蜈蚣的腳痛。）

· centipede [`sɛntəpid] *n.* 蜈蚣

→ 長頸鹿的脖子長，喉嚨痛是很糟的事；蜈蚣腳多，當然腳痛更糟。

A centipede with sore feet is worse than a giraffe with a sore throat.

6 Q: What is worse than raining cats and dogs?

（什麼比下貓下狗更糟／傾盆大雨更糟？）

A: Hailing lions and tigers. （下雹獅和虎。）

‧ hail [hel] *n.* 雹；*v.* 冰雹，大聲招呼

例 It's hailing outside. （外面在下雹。）

I will hail a cab for you. （我會為你叫計程車。）

本題中有「傾盆大雨」一詞，請參看 4 (1)，我們可用進行式寫出："It is raining cats and dogs." 字譯：下貓下狗；正在大雨如注。仿上句，將 "rain" 換成 "hail"，將 "cats and dogs" 換成 "lions and tigers"："It is hailing lions and tigers."。

7 Q: What is better than "to give credit where credit is due"?

（什麼比「給信用予那些該予以信用的人」還要更好？）

A: Give cash. （給現金。）

→ to give credit where credit is due 表揚那些該予以表揚的

讓我們逐字說明：credit [`krɛdɪt] *n.* 賒購方式；信用；信任；功勞；增光的人 (或事物)；學分。例：

I can't afford to pay cash, I would like to buy the car on credit.

(我無法付現金，我想用賒購方式買車)。

現今最流行的是信用卡 (credit card)，購物不必付現金，刷卡即可。刷卡購物相當於賒購方式，先享用後付款，不過這牽涉到個人信用問題。例：

Her credit is good. She has a good credit-rating.

(她的信用良好。她有很好的信譽評價。)

Do you place any credit in his saying? (你信任他的說法嗎？)

He is trying to claim credit for the invention.

(他正要把這項發明說成是自己的功勞。)

He is a credit to our team. (他是我們隊的光榮。)

He has enough credits to get his degree. (他有足夠的學分獲得學位。)

‧ due [dju] *adj.* 應給的，應歸於的，應得的；到期的

例 Our grateful thanks are due to Purdue University for their help in the making of this film.

（我們由衷感謝普渡大學在製作這部影片的過程中所給予我們的協助。）

字譯：「我們由衷的感謝應歸於普渡大學在…的協助。」

The bill is due today. （這帳單今天到期。）

The homework is due next Tuesday. （交作業的期限是下週二。）

→ 從上面的例句可看出 "due" 一字的用法，我們寫一句跟謎題有直接關聯的句子： "We must give credit where it is due." 句中的 it 指 credit，字譯：「在應給讚揚之處我們必須給讚揚。」 意即「我們必須表揚那些該予以表揚的人。」 若把 "credit" 作「信用」解，則上句可譯為：「我們必須將信用給那些該予以信用的人。」 現在我們回頭看謎題中 "to give credit where credit is due" 之真正涵義是「給信用予那些該予以信用的人。」

(26) *Dictionary Nations*

以 "Nation"（國家）作為字尾的字很多，所以很容易以 nation 做謎題。例如：

「學生最怕什麼 nation？」謎底是 "Examination"。「什麼是虛幻的 nation？」謎底是 "imagination"。

現在讓我們來看看有關於 Nation 的謎題：

1 Q: What nation is a dislike nation?（什麼 nation 是討厭的 nation？）

A: Abomination.（厭惡。）

· abomination [ə͵bɑmə`neʃən] *n.* 厭惡，憎恨

2 Q: What nation is a bewildered nation?（什麼 nation 是迷惑的 nation？）

A: Consternation.（驚愕。）

· consternation [͵kɑnstə`neʃən] *n.* 驚恐；驚惶失措

例 I was filled with consternation to hear that she was ill.

（我聽說她病了，感到很震驚。）

3 Q: What nation is at the peak?（什麼 nation 在顛峰？）

A: Culmination.（極點，頂點。）

· culmination [͵kʌlmə`neʃən] *n.* 頂點，極點

例 The publish of this book is the culmination of my life's work.

（這本書的出版是我一生工作的頂點。）

4 Q: What nation is a fortune-telling nation?

（什麼 nation 是相命的 nation？）

A: Divination.（卜卦。）

· divination [͵dɪvə`neʃən] *n.* 卜卦；預言

5 Q: What nation is a religious nation?（什麼 nation 是宗教的 nation？）

A: Denomination.（教派。）

- denomination [dɪˌnamə`neʃən] *n.* 宗派，教派

6 Q : What nation is one of the most resolute nation?

（什麼 nation 是最有決心的 nation 之一？）

A : Determination.（決心。）

- determination [dɪˌtɝmə`neʃən] *n.* 決斷力，決心

例 He spoke of his determination to study English well.

（他談到他決心要把英文學好。）

7 Q : What nation is one that travelers often want?

（什麼 nation 是旅行者經常所需要的？）

A : Destination.（目的地。）

- destination [ˌdɛstə`neʃən] *n.* 目的地，終點；收件人的地址

例 I am bound for Taipei, that is my destination.

（我要到臺北去，那是我的目的地。）

8 Q : What nation scatters things far and wide?

（什麼 nation 把東西散佈得又遠又廣？）

A : Dissemination.（散佈。）

- dissemination [dɪˌsɛmə`neʃən] *n.* 散佈，傳播（消息、思想等）

9 Q : What nation is a tyrant?（什麼 nation 是暴君？）

A : Domination.（統治。）

- domination [ˌdamə`neʃən] *n.* 控制，統治；優勢

例 We struggled for the domination of the country.

（我們為取得對這個國家的控制而奮鬥。）

10 Q : What is a very unfair nation?（什麼是非常不公平的 nation？）

A : Discrimination.（歧視。）

- discrimination [dɪˌskrɪmə`neʃən] *n.* 歧視，排斥

例 I hate the discrimination against women.（我憎恨對婦女的歧視。）

⑪ Q：What nation is dreaded by school boys?

（什麼 nation 最為學童們所懼怕？）

A：Examination.（考試。）

・examination [ɪɡ͵zæmə`neʃən] *n.* 考試

例 The students are afraid of examination.

（學生怕考試。）

Before we offer you the job, you must have a medical examination.

（在我們提供你工作之前，你必須做身體檢查。）

examination

⑫ Q：What nation is a teacher's nation?

（什麼 nation 是老師的 nation？）

A：Explanation.（解釋。）

・explanation [͵ɛksplə`neʃən] *n.* 解釋；說明

例 He offered no explanation for his absence.（他沒提供他缺席的說明。）

⑬ Q：What nation produces the greatest number of marriages?

（什麼 nation 產生最多的姻緣？）

A：Fascination.（吸引力。）

・fascination [͵fæsṇ`eʃən] *n.* 吸引力

例 Chinese art has a great fascination for me.

（中國藝術對我有非常大的吸引力。）

⑭ Q：What nation is a crazy nation?（什麼 nation 是瘋狂的 nation？）

A：Hallucination.（幻覺。）

・hallucination [hə͵lusṇ`eʃən] *n.* 幻覺

⑮ Q：What nation is a fanciful nation?（什麼 nation 是空想的 nation？）

A：Imagination.（想像。）

- image [ˋɪmɪʤ] *n.* 影像
- imagine [ɪˋmæʤɪn] *v.* 想像
- imaginary [ɪˋmæʤə‚nɛrɪ] *adj.* 想像的
- imagination [ɪ‚mæʤəˋneʃən] *n.* 想像力；想像

16 Q: What nation is a leaning nation?（什麼 nation 是傾斜的 nation？）

A: Inclination.（傾斜。）

- inclination [‚ɪnkləˋneʃən] *n.* 傾向，趨勢

17 Q: What nation is a disrespectful nation?

（什麼 nation 是不恭敬的 nation？）

A: Insubordination.（不順從。）

- subordination [sə‚bɔrdnˋeʃən] *n.* 順從
- insubordination [‚ɪnsə‚bɔrdnˋeʃən] *n.* 不順從
- respectful [rɪˋspɛktfəl] *adj.* 恭敬的
- disrespectful [‚dɪsrɪˋspɛktfəl] *adj.* 不恭敬的

我們可仿這謎題自己做一個：

Q: What nation is a respectful nation?（什麼 nation 是恭敬的 nation？）

A: Subordination.（順從。）

18 Q: What nation is a dramatic nation?（什麼 nation 是戲劇的 nation？）

A: Impersonation.（扮演。）

- impersonation [‚ɪmpɝsn̩ˋeʃən] *n.* 扮演

例 He does a marvellous impersonation of the doctor.（他演醫生演得很好。）

19 Q: What nation is a very bright nation?

（什麼 nation 是十分光明的 nation？）

A: Illumination.（照明。）

- illumination [ɪ‚luməˋneʃən] *n.* 照明

例 The illumination is too weak here.（這裡的照明太弱。）

⑳ Q: What nation is a scheming nation?（什麼 nation 是陰謀的 nation？）

A: Machination.（陰謀。）

· machination [ˌmækəˋneʃən] *n.* 陰謀，詭計

· scheme [skim] *v.* 搞陰謀

例 They have been scheming to hurt me.（他們一直處心積慮想傷害我。）

→ scheming 為 scheme 的現在分詞，可作形容詞用：搞陰謀的。

例 I have never trusted that scheming bastard.

（我從不相信那專搞陰謀的壞蛋。）

> 禮運大同篇中：「謀閉而不興。」中的「謀閉」就是「不軌的圖謀」，"Evil scheming is repressed." 禮運大同篇的譯文請參見附錄 G

(27) *Name the Nations*

　　以國家作為謎題，或以國家名稱作為謎底，例如：那一國很嚴寒？謎底是 **Chile**（智利），因為 **Chile** 的發音與 chilly 相同；chilly 寒冷，故答案為 **Chile**。

　　現在讓我們來看看有關國家的謎題：

1 Q : What country is useful at meal time?（什麼國家在用餐時是有用的？）

　　A : China.（中國。）

　　→ china 亦作「瓷器」解，但須小寫。

2 Q : What country is good for skaters?（什麼國家對溜冰者是有益的？）

　　A : Iceland.（冰島。）

　　→ land (土地) 上有 ice 才能溜冰。

3 Q : What country is a coin?（什麼國家是一枚硬幣？）

　　A : Guinea.（幾內亞。）

　　· **guinea** [ˋɡɪnɪ] *n.* 畿尼（舊時英國金幣，合 **1.05** 英鎊）

4 Q : What country suggests a straw hat?（什麼國家代表草帽？）

　　A : Panama.（巴拿馬。）

　　→ 巴拿馬草帽世界聞名，稱為 Panama hat。

5 Q : What country expresses anger?（什麼國家表示忿怒？）

　　A : Ireland.（愛爾蘭。）

　　· **ire** [aɪr] *n.* 憤怒

6 Q : What country mourns?（什麼國家悲哀？）

　　A : Wales.（威爾斯。）

7 Q : What country has a good appetite?（什麼國家有好胃口？）

　　A : Hungary.（匈牙利。）

　　→ Hungary 與 hungry (飢餓的) 讀音相近。

8 **Q** : What country is popular on Thanksgiving Day?

（什麼國家在感恩節受人歡迎？）

A : Turkey.（土耳其。）

→ turkey 亦作「火雞」解。美國在感恩節有火雞宴。

9 **Q** : What country does the cook use?（什麼國家廚師會用到？）

A : Greece.（希臘。）

→ Greece (希臘) 與 grease (脂肪) 同音。

· **Greek** [grik] *n.* 希臘文

據説世界三大最難語文是中文、俄文和希臘文。英文有一句話："It's all Greek to me." 字譯：對我而言都是希臘文，真正涵義是「於我如天書」意思是「完全看不懂」或「不知所書。」

---

10 **Q** : What country is very cold?（什麼國家非常冷？）

A : Chile.（智利。）

→ Chile 與 chilly 發音相同。

· **chilly** [ˋʧɪlɪ] *adj.* 嚴寒的

What country is very cold?

28 *Miss Trees/Mysteries*

Miss Trees（樹小姐）與 Mysteries（神祕，mystery 之複數形）二者讀音相近。有很多謎題以樹為謎底，例如「什麼樹好吻？」謎底是 tulip（鬱金香），因 tulip 與 "two lips"（雙唇）讀音相近之故。

現在讓我們來看看有關樹的謎底：

1 Q：What trees are left behind after a fire?（火燒之後什麼樹會留下來？）

A：Ashes.（梣／灰燼。）

→ 火燒之後，僅剩灰燼 (ash)。

2 Q：What tree is an inlet of the sea?（什麼樹是海的進口？）

A：Bay.（月桂樹／港灣。）

3 Q：What tree grows at the seaside?（什麼樹生長在海邊？）

A：Beech.（櫸木／海灘。）

→ beech (櫸木) 與 beach (海灘) 同音。

4 Q：What tree is a fish?（什麼樹是一種魚？）

A：Bass.（菩提樹。）

・ bass [bæs] *n.* 鱸魚

5 Q：What tree is like an old joke?（什麼樹像一個老笑話？）

A：Chestnut.（栗樹。）

・ chestnut [ˋtʃɛsnət] *n.* 老掉牙的笑話；陳腔濫調

例 He always tells chestnuts.（他老是講些老掉牙的笑話。）

6 Q：What tree is often found in the bottles?（什麼樹可常在瓶子裡找到？）

A：Cork.（軟木樹／軟木塞。）

7 Q：What is the most important of all the trees in history?

（歷史上最重要的樹是什麼？）

A : Date.（棗樹。）

→ date 亦作「日期」解。

⑧ **Q** : What tree is older than most other trees?（什麼樹比其他樹都老？）

A : Elder.（接骨木。）

→ elder 亦作「長者」解。

⑨ **Q** : What tree is an awful grouch?（什麼樹的脾氣最壞？）

A : Crab.（山查子樹／牢騷。）

⑩ **Q** : What tree is often found in people's mouths?

（什麼樹常在人們的口裡找到？）

A : Gum.（橡膠樹。）

· **gum** [gʌm] *n.* 牙床，牙齦

例 Massage your gums after brushing your teeth.（刷牙後，按摩牙床。）

⑪ **Q** : What tree is a kind of grasshopper?（什麼樹是一種蚱蜢？）

A : Locust.（刺槐／蝗蟲或蚱蜢。）

⑫ **Q** : What tree does everyone carry in his hand?（什麼樹每個人拿在手裡？）

A : Palm.（棕櫚樹。）

· **palm** [pɑm] *n.* 手掌

palm

A palm in the palm.

注意發音，l 不發音。有很多字中的 l 是不發音的。請參見附錄 H

⑬ **Q**: What tree is a good-looking girl?（什麼樹是美貌的女孩子？）

A: Peach.（桃樹）

→ peach 亦作「美人」解。

> 國人看美人，形容成「像水蜜桃」，有名的成語「人面桃花」也與美人有關。謂某人走桃花運，亦有一桃字，桃與美人有關聯。在這方面，中西觀念是一樣的。

⑭ **Q**: What tree is a carpenter's tool?（什麼樹是木匠的工具？）

A: Plane.（梧桐。）

→ plane 亦作「刨床」解。

⑮ **Q**: What tree is always longing for someone?（什麼樹總是在思念別人？）

A: Pine.（松樹。）

⑯ **Q**: What tree is one of your parents?（什麼樹是你的雙親之一？）

A: Pawpaw (papa).（番木瓜樹〔爸爸〕。）

→ pawpaw 與 papa 讀音相近。

⑰ **Q**: What tree always is two people?（什麼樹總是兩個人？）

A: Pear (pair).（梨樹〔一雙〕。）

→ pear (梨樹) 與 pair (一雙) 同音。

⑱ **Q**: What tree is the straightest tree?（什麼樹長得最直？）

A: Plum (plumb).（李樹〔垂直〕。）

→ plum (李樹) 與 plumb (垂直) 同音。plumb 中的 b 不發音。

⑲ **Q**: What tree always has a neat appearance?

　　（什麼樹總是有整潔的外貌？）

A: Spruce.（雲杉。）

· spruce [sprus] *n.* 雲杉 *adj.* 整潔漂亮的

例 He looks very spruce in his new suit.（他穿上新西裝看上去很帥。）

⑳ **Q**: What trees are nice to kiss?（什麼樹很好吻？）

A: Tulip (two lips).（鬱金香〔兩片唇〕。）

→ tulip 與 two lips 讀音相近，僅差一個字母 s。

21 Q: What tree is always very sad?（什麼樹總是悲哀？）

A: Weeping willow.（垂柳。）

→ "weeping willow" 亦可作「哭泣的楊柳」解。

> 國人形容柳樹為「楊柳依依」，柳樹因風起，婆娑起舞，婀娜多姿。但美國人看柳枝下垂，如人垂頭喪氣，故謂之「哭泣的柳樹」(weeping willow) 中國人和西方人在這方面的觀念是不一樣的。

22 Q: What tree run over the meadows and pastures?

（什麼樹在草地和牧場跑來跑去？）

A: Yew (ewe).（紫杉樹〔母羊〕。）

- yew [ju] *n.* 紫杉樹
- ewe [ju] *n.* 母羊

23 Q: What tree goes into ladies' winter coats?

（什麼樹在女人冬天的大衣裡？）

A: Fir (fur).（樅樹〔軟毛〕。）

- fir [fɝ] *n.* 樅，冷衫
- fur [fɝ] *n.* 軟毛（例如貓身上的軟毛）

29 *The Riddle of Sphinx*

The Riddle of the Sphinx is probably the oldest of all riddles. It appears in ancient Greek mythology.

（斯芬克士謎語也許是所有謎語中最古老的一個。它出自古希臘神話。）

The Sphinx, a monster with a human head and the body of a beast, sat on a high rock by the roadside near the city of Thebes, in Egypt. To everyone who passed by she asked the following riddle:

（斯芬克士是一個人面獸身的怪物，牠坐在底比斯城附近路旁的高高岩石上，向每個過路的人問下面的謎語：）

"What is it that has but one voice, and goes first on four feet, then on two, and lastly on three?"

（「什麼東西只有一種聲音，起初用四隻腳走路，然後用兩隻腳，最後用三隻腳？」）

All who could not solve the riddle were strangled by the Sphinx and then thrown down from the high rock. For a long time nobody could guess the answer, and a great many people were killed. （答不出謎底的人都被斯芬克士勒死，然後摔到岩石下。很久無人能猜中答案，許多人因此喪生。）

Finally, Oedipus, the son of the king of Thebes, came along the road and was stopped by the Sphinx. The Sphinx asked him the famous riddle.

（最後，底比斯國王的兒子伊底帕斯路過該地，斯芬克士把他擋下，問他這個著名的謎語。）

Said Oedipus, "The answer to your riddle is a man."

（伊底帕斯說：「你的謎底是人。」）

"What makes you think that?" demanded the Sphinx.

（「你怎麼會認為那樣？」斯芬克士要求說明。）

"Because a man crawls on all fours as an infant, then walks erect on two feet, and in his old age uses a staff or a cane." Oedipus replied.

（「因為人在嬰兒時用四肢爬，然後直起身來用兩隻腳走路，年老時用枴杖或藤條。」伊底帕斯答道。）

What goes first on four feets, then on two, and lastly on three?

This was indeed the right answer. The Sphinx was so furious when her riddle was solved that she threw herself down from the high rock and perished, but her riddle has lasted throughout the centuries, and still puzzles a lot of people, even today.

（這就是正確的答案。當謎底揭穿之後，斯芬克士憤怒異常，於是牠從高高的岩石上縱身一跳，摔下身亡。不過牠的謎語仍世代相傳，即使至今，仍然使很多人困惑。）

- mythology [ˌmɪˈθɑlədʒɪ] *n.* 神話
- monster [ˈmɑnstɚ] *n.* 怪物
- strangle [ˈstræŋgl̩] *v.* 勒死，使窒息
- crawl [ˈkrɔl] *v.* 爬行
- infant [ˈɪnfənt] *n.* 嬰兒
- staff [stæf] *n.* 棍棒

- cane [ken] *n.* 藤條，手杖
- furious [`fjurɪəs] *adj.* 憤怒的
- perish [`pɛrɪʃ] *v.* 毀滅，死亡
- century [`sɛntʃərɪ] *n.* 世紀
- puzzle [`pʌzl̩] *v.* 困惑
- thrown [θron] *n. v.* (throw/ threw/ thrown) 拋，擲，扔

30 *Riddles in Rhyme*

　　謎語押韻，有如詩詞。中文謎題多押韻，唸起來順口，聽起來順耳。例如：「園中花已化去，夕陽一點已西墜。相思淚，心已碎，空轉馬蹄歸。秋紅已殘，螢火已飛。」猜一姓氏。謎底是「蘇」。英文謎語也有押韻的，別有一番風味。

　　現在讓我們來看看有關押韻的謎語：

1 **Q**：A houseful, a roomful,

　　Can't catch a spoonful?

　　（滿屋子，滿房間，

　　卻裝不滿一湯匙？）

A：smoke.（煙。）

2 **Q**：Up and down, up and down,

　　Touching neither sky nor ground.

　　（上上下下，上上下下，

　　不觸天也不碰地。）

A：A pump handle.（泵的柄。）

3 **Q**：Though I dance at a ball,

　　I am nothing at all.

　　（雖然在舞會上起舞，

　　但我卻飄渺虛無。）

A：A shadow.（影子。）

4 **Q**：You can press your attire,

　　When I contact a wire.

　　（當我接上電線，

　　你就可以壓平你的服裝。）

A : An electric iron.（電熨斗。）

5 Q : No need for brush, no need for broom,

I'm used a lot to tidy a room.

（不需刷子，不需帚，

清理房間由我做。）

A : A vacuum cleaner.（真空吸塵器。）

6 Q : I tremble at each breath of air,

And yet the heaviest burdens bear.

（輕輕吹口氣，我就會顫抖，

卻可承受最重的負擔。）

A : Water.（水。）

7 Q : Round as a biscuit, busy as a bee,

Prettiest little thing you ever did see.

（圓如餅，忙如蜂，

你所見過最美的小東西。）

A : A watch.（錶。）

→ 手錶一般呈圓形，像小圓餅。不停的走，忙如蜜蜂。

8 Q : The mother of men was a lady whose name,

Read backward or forward, is always the same.

（是人的母親也是女人的名字，

倒唸或順唸都如是。）

A : Eve.（夏娃。）

9 Q : Thirty-two white horses on a red hill, now they go and now they

stand still.

（三十二匹白馬在紅色的山丘上，

時而站立，時而奔走。）

A : Your teeth. (你的牙齒。)

→ 牙齒通常上下排各十六顆，共三十二顆，顏色是白的，紅色山丘代表牙齦。不吃東西或閉嘴時，站著不動。說話或吃東西時，上下奔走。

10 Q : If a well-known animal you behead, another one you will have instead. (你把一個眾所周知的動物的頭斬掉，你就會得到另一種動物。)

A : Fox. (狐狸。)

→ 將 Fox 斬首，去掉 F，即得 ox (公牛)！

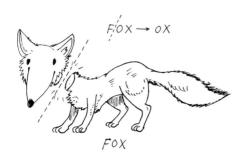
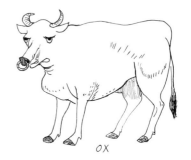

If a fox beheaded, it becomes an ox.

11 Q : What is it you can touch, and also you can feel;

It has neither size nor shape,

But just the same, it's real.

（接觸得到，感覺得到；

既無大小，又無形狀，

但無論怎麼說，它是真實的。）

A : The air. (空氣。)

→ 題中 just the same 為轉接語，相當於 by the way；on the other hand，切不可字譯。

⑫ Q : It wasn't my sister, nor my brother,

But still was the child of my father and mother,

Who was it?

（非我姊妹，非我兄弟，

但仍是我父母的孩子，

那是誰？）

A : Myself.（我自己。）

→ 既無兄弟，又無姊妹，就是獨子 (only son)，又是爸媽的孩子，當然是自己。

⑬ Q : Little Nanny Etticote, in a white petticoat,

Holding up a bright red rose;

The longer she stands,

The shorter she grows.

（小小蘭妮，身著白色小外衣，

舉著鮮紅色的玫瑰；

她站得越久，

就變得越矮。）

A : A candle.（蠟燭。）

→ 紅玫瑰是指燭火，蠟燭立在那裡燒越久，會越燒越短。

⑭ Q : I tell heat, and I tell cold,

And they in turn tell me to go up and down as I am told.

They tell me; I agree.

（我報熱，我報冷，

冷熱也回頭告訴我，

熱冷告訴我時上上下下。

是熱是冷，我同意。）

A : The mercury in a thermometer.（溫度計裡的水銀。）

⑮ Q：Great number do our use despise,

But yet, at last they find,

Without our help in many things,

They might as well be blind.

（很多人輕視我們的用處，

但是，最後他們發現，

若沒有我們的幫助，

很多東西他們都看不見。）

　A：A pair of spectacles.（眼鏡。）

⑯ Q：I often murmur, but never weep;

Lie in bed, but never sleep;

My mouth is larger than my head,

In spite of the fact I'm never fed;

I have no feet, yet swiftly run;

The more falls I get, move faster on.

（我常低聲哀怨，但從不哭泣；

躺在床上，但從不睡覺；

雖然我從不餵食，

我的嘴卻比頭大；

我沒腳，卻跑得快；

摔倒越多，運動的越快。）

　A：A river.（河流。）

(31) *Rhymed Charades*

rhyme [raɪm] 韻文，rhymed [raɪmd] 押韻的，charade [ʃəˋred] 文字謎，rhymed charade 即押韻的文字謎。顧名思義，它是謎題，而唸起來又押韻，和詩詞一樣。以下有若干押韻文字謎，供讀者欣賞。雖然各謎題皆有譯文，但並未譯成韻文，對英文造詣較深的讀者不妨一試。

現在讓我們來看看有關押韻的文字謎：

1⃝ Q: My first is with bee,

My second rules the sea.

My whole I would spend with thee.

What am I?

（我的第一部分與蜜蜂在一起，

我的第二部分支配海洋。

我的整體我將與你共度。

我是什麼？）

honeymoon

A: Honeymoon.（蜜月。）

→ 與 bee 在一起的是 honey。能支配海洋，造成潮汐的是 moon。honey 和 moon 合在一起就成了 honeymoon。honeymoon 當然要與心愛的人共度。

2⃝ Q: My first is a tool,

My second a coin;

My whole is speech that's something annoying.

（我的第一部分是工具，

第二部分是硬幣；

整體是一種令人厭煩的語言。）

A: Accent (Ax-cent).（口音〔斧———一分硬幣〕。）

→ accent 亦作「重音」解。Ax-cent 與 accent 讀音相同。

③ Q：My first is what,

My second is not,

And my whole you put in a corner.

（第一部分是 **what**，

第二部分是 **not**，

我的整體你把它放在角落。）

A：A whatnot.（陳列書籍或裝飾物等的架子。）

④ Q：My first I hope you are,

My second I see you are,

My whole I know you are.

（我希望你是我的第一部分，

我看到你是我的第二部分，

我知道你是我的整體。）

A：Welcome (well-come).（歡迎〔好——來〕。）

→ 謎底是："I hope you are well. I see you are coming. I know you are welcome."

⑤ Q：My first of anything is half,

My second is complete;

And so remains until once more,

My first and second meet.

（我第一部分是一半，

第二部分是完整的；

直到我第一和第二部分相遇，

一直是如此。）

A：Semi-circle.（半圓。）

→ semi 作「半」解，例如 semi conductor，半導體；semi lunar，半月形的。

6 Q : My first is a circle,

My second a cross,

If you meet with my whole,

Look out for a toss.

（第一部分是圓，

第二部分是叉，

如果遇到我的整體，

小心遭到頂撞。）

A : Ox.（公牛。）

→ Ox 的第一部分是圓 (O)，第二部分是叉 (X)，合起來是 ox。注意 ox 頭會頂撞。

‧ **toss** [tɔs] *n.* 投擲；震盪

7 Q : Without my first you'd look very strange,

My second we all want to be;

My whole is what many a lady has worn

At a dance or a party or tea.

（沒有我的第一部分你會看來奇怪，

我們都希望是第二部分；在舞會或宴

會或用茶時很多婦人戴我的整體。）

A : Nose-gay.（花束，花球。）

→ Without nose you'd look very strange.

We all want to be gay (快樂).

8 Q : My first is a part of the day,

My last a conductor of light;

My whole to take measure of time

Is usually by day and by night.

（我的第一部分是一天的一部分，

最後部分可導光；

我的整體可計時，

日夜不停止。）

A : Hourglass.（滴漏。）

→ 滴漏為用滴下的沙或水計時的器具。

⑨ Q : My first some gladly take entirely for my second's sake;

But few, indeed, will ever care both together ever to bear.

（有些人樂於得到我的第一部分完全是為了第二部分的緣故；

但兩者合併卻很少人願意擔負。）

A : Misfortune (Miss-fortune).（不幸〔小姐——財產〕。）

→ misfortune (不幸) 與 Miss-fortune (小姐——財產) 發音相同。有些人想得到一位

小姐，是因她有 fortune 的緣故，但將 miss 和 fortune 合併在一起，成了

misfortune (不幸) 就很少人願意去擔負了。

⑩ Q : My first is what you're doing now,

My second is obtained from stone;

Before my whole you often stand,

But mostly when you're all alone.

（你正在做我的第一部分，

第二部分取之於石頭；

你常站在我的整體前面，

但大多是在你單獨時。）

A : Looking-glass.（鏡子。）

32 *Enigmas*

Q: I'm not in the earth, nor the sun, nor the moon.

You may search all the sky—I'm not there.

In the morning and evening—though not in the noon.

You may plainly perceive me, for, like a balloon.

I am midway suspended in air.

Though disease may possess me, and sickness and pain.

I am never in sorrow nor gloom;

Though in wit and in wisdom

I equally reign,

I'm the heart of all sin and have long lived in vain;

Yet I never shall be found in the tomb.

(This is a famous enigma written by Lord Byron.)

我不在地球，不在太陽，也不在月亮上。

任你尋遍整個天空，我也不在那方。

雖然不在正午，但在早上和晚上。

我像氣球般懸在半空，你能看到我的真相。

縱然被疾病、病痛和苦楚糾纏，

但我決不憂愁也不悲傷；

雖然我才智雙全，

卻是萬惡的中心，在人生的旅途我枉走了這一趟。

不過我決不會出現在墓場。

——拜倫

A: The letter I.（字母 I。）

→ 這個謎題是有趣的文字遊戲。earth, sun 和 moon 中沒有字母 i。本來第一句後面還可多加 nor the star，但為了押韻 (moon, noon, balloon)，所以不能多加 northe star。整個 sky 裡也沒有 i，但在 morning 和 evening 中有。但 noon 中無 i。懸掛在半空 (air) 中，i 在 air 的中央。disease、sickness 和 pain 中有 i；sorrow 和 gloom 中沒有 i。wit 和 wisdom 中有 i。sin 的中央字母是 i，lived in vain 字譯為住在 vain 中 (vain 中有 i)，但 in vain 是作「枉然」解。在 tomb 中也找不到 i。

② Q: The beginning of eternity.

   The end of time and space.

   The beginning of every end,

   The end of every place.

   是永恆的開始。

   是時間和空間的結尾。

   是每個結尾的開端，

   是每個地方的結尾。

A: The letter E.（字母 E。）

→ eternity 的字首為 e，time 和 space 的字尾為 e，end 及 place 的字尾也為 e。

③ Q: I have wings yet never fly,

   I have sails yet never go,

   I can't keep still if I try,

   Yet forever stand just so.

   我有翼卻不飛翔，

   有帆卻不遠航，

   我欲靜卻無從而靜，

   永遠是站立模樣。

A: A windmill.（風車。）

④ Q: Two heads I have and strange as it may be,

I can be found in every big army,

I'm always still except when roughly used,

But I can be noisy when beaten or abused.

Soldiers of all nations rely on me,

So I can be useful, as you can see.

說來奇怪我有兩個頭，

在每個大軍中都能找到我，

若非待我鹵莽，我總是寂靜無聲，

但當敲擊或亂打我時，我就嘈雜喧囂。

各國士兵都需要我，所以你知道我的用途大。

A : A drum. (鼓。)

→ 鼓的兩面稱為 head。

· abuse [əˋbjus] *v.* 濫用

· beaten [ˋbitn̩] *v.* (beat/ beat/ beaten) 打

⑤ Q : We are familiar little creatures,

　　Each has different forms and features.

　　One of us in a glass is set,

　　Another you will find in jet;

　　A third you'll find if you look in tin,

　　And forth, a beautiful box within;

　　And the fifth, if you pursue,

　　It will never fly from you.

　　我們是大家熟悉的小生物，

　　各有不同的形體和特徵。

　　我們之中有一個安置在玻璃中，

　　另一個在噴射機中可找到，

　　在錫裡你可找到第三個，

　　第四個放在漂亮的盒子中；

　　你若追求第五個，

　　它決不會離你飛走。

A : The vowels-A, E, I, O and U. (母音 A，E，I，O 和 U。)

→ 五個母音 A, E, I, O 和 U 正好在 glass, jet, tin, box 和 you 的中間。

⑥ Q : I am a caller at every home that you may meet,

　　For daily I make my way along each street;

　　Take one letter from me and still you will see

　　I'm the same as before, as I always will be;

　　Take two letters from me, or three or four,

　　I'll still be the same as I was before.

　　In fact, I'll say that all my letters you may take.

　　Yet of me nothing else you'll make.

我是你遇到的每家訪客，

每天我都通過每條街；

拿走我一個字母／投遞了一封信，

你會覺得我與以往無異。

拿走我兩個字母／投遞兩封信，或三個或四個，

我仍與以前沒有兩樣。

事實上，即使你拿走我所有的字母／信。

你也無法把我變成其他的東西。

A： A postman.（郵差。）

7 Q： My first is in pork, but not in ham;

My second is in oyster, but not in clam;

My third is in pond, but not in lake;

My fourth is in hand, but not in shake;

My fifth is in eye, but not in pink;

My whole is a flower, you'll guess if you think.

我的第一個字母在豬肉中，但不在火腿裡；

第二個字母在牡蠣中，但不在蛤蜊；

第三個字母在池塘中，但不在湖中；

第四個字母在手中，但不在握手中；

第五個字母在眼中，但不在小鮭魚中；

我的全部是一朵花，你若想想就能猜到它。

A : Peony.（牡丹花）

→ 這五個字母正好在 pork, oyster, pond, hand 和 eye 中。

⑧ Q : Just equal are my head and tail,

My middle slender as can be,

Whether I stand on head or heel,

'Tis all the same to you and me.

But if my head should be cut off,

The matter's true, although 'tis strange,

My head and body, severed thus,

Immediately to nothing change.

我首尾相同，

腰部〔中央〕苗條無比，

無論正立或倒立，

對你我都無異。

但若將我斬首，雖屬離奇，

你會發現我的頭與身體相去無幾。

A : The figure 8.（數字 8。）

→ "8" 字首尾相同。腰部很纖細。正立或倒立都是 8。若將 8 字從中切開，頭與身體皆為 0，故相去無幾。

③③ *Tongue Twisters*

　　多練習繞口令 **(tongue twister)** 對發音及說話的流暢度有很大的幫助，讀者可勤加練習，其樂無比。

　　現在讓我們來看看有關英文的繞口令：

① I lend ten men ten hens.（我借給十個男人十隻母雞。）

　　→ 這句繞口令都是 [ɛn] 音，不會太難唸。

② She sells sea shells by the sea shore.

　　If she sells sea shells by the sea shore,

　　Where are the sea shells she sells by the sea shore?

　　她在海岸邊賣海貝殼。

　　如果她在海岸邊賣海貝殼，

　　何處是她在海岸邊賣的海貝殼？

　　→ 這段繞口令可練習 [s] 與 [ʃ] 的發音。

③ Of all the saws I ever saw, I never saw a saw saw like this saw saws.

　　在我所見過的鋸子中，我從未見過一把鋸子鋸東西像這把鋸子鋸的如此。

　　→ 這句中有七個 "saw"，saw 是 see 的過去式，saw 也作「鋸子」解，當動詞用時，作「鋸」解。

④ How much wood would a woodchuck chuck?

　　If a woodchuck could chuck wood?

　　He would chuck as much wood as a woodchuck could

　　If a woodchuck could chuck wood.

　　如果土撥鼠能夠撥弄木頭，

　　那麼土撥鼠會撥弄多少木頭？

　　如果土撥鼠真能撥弄木頭，

土撥鼠就會盡土撥鼠所能撥弄一樣多的木頭。

→ 這段繞口令的主要發音是 [u] 音。

- wood [wud] *n.* 木頭
- could [kud] *aux.* 能；可以
- would [wud] *aux.* 將；大概

5 I am not the big fig plucker nor the big fig plucker's son,

but I'll pluck big figs till the big fig plucker comes.

我既不是摘大無花果的人，也不是摘大無花果人的兒子，

但是我要摘大無花果，一直摘到摘大無花果人到來。

→ 這段繞口令的關鍵字在 big fig plucker，唸起來有 b、f、p 的音，相當拗口。

6 How many sheets should a sheet—slitter slit

If a sheet—slitter should slit sheets?

He should slit as many sheets as a sheet—slitter should,

If a sheet—slitter should slit sheets.

假如一個裁被單的人要裁被單，

那麼一個裁被單的人該裁多少被單？

假如一個裁被單的人要裁被單，

他會盡可能裁得像一個裁被單的人所該裁的那麼多。

→ 這段繞口令與第(4)題的結構相似，將 how many 改為 how much，should 改為 would，slit 改為 chuck，as many 改為 as much。

- sheet [ʃit] *n.* 被單；一張
- slitter [ˋslɪtɚ] *n.* 割裂者
- slit [slɪt] *v.* (slit/ slit/ slit) 割裂，裁開

7 Fuzzy Wuzzy was a bear.

Fuzzy Wuzzy had no hair.

Fuzzy Wuzzy wasn't fuzzy, was he (Wuzzy)?

毛絨絨的 **Wuzzy** 是頭熊。

毛絨絨的 **Wuzzy** 沒頭髮。

毛絨絨的 **Wuzzy** 並不毛絨絨，是嗎？

· fuzzy [`fʌzɪ] *adj.* 模糊的，毛絨絨的

→ 形容貓身上的毛是毛絨絨的用 "fuzzy" 一字。Wuzzy 乃動物名。"was he" 與 "Wuzzy" 音相近。若將 "was he" 唸快，則與 "Wuzzy" 同音。

8 Round and round the rugged rocks a ragged rascal ran.

一個衣衫襤褸的流氓繞著凹凸不平的岩石跑。

9 Peter Piper picked a peck of pickled peppers;

A peck of pickled peppers Peter Piper picked.

If Peter Piper picked a peck of pickled peppers,

Where's the peck of pickled peppers Peter Piper picked?

彼得派波揀了一配克醃辣椒；

一配克醃辣椒彼得派波揀到了。

如果彼得派波揀了一配克醃辣椒，

何處是彼得派波揀的那一配克醃辣椒？

→ 這段繞口令的關鍵音是 [pi]，[pɪ]，[pɛ]，[paɪ]，非常拗口，想唸得快又順，並非易事。

· peck [pɛk] *n.* 配克（容量單位）

· pickle [pɪkl̩] *v.* 醃漬

· pickled pepper 醃的辣椒

· Peter [`pitɚ] 彼得（名）

· Piper [`paɪpɚ] 派波（姓）

這幾句話使我憶起小時候唸的繞口令：

「廟裡鼓，鼓破用布補，是鼓補布？還是布補鼓？」

「棚上瓶碰破棚下盆，是瓶碰盆？還是盆碰瓶？」

附錄

附錄 A

River Road

River Road, River Road, winding to the sea.

That's the road leading home where I long to be.

Long to see folks I knew, friends of long ago.

Long to sit by my door in the sunset glow.

River Road. River Road, winding to the sea.

Load the way take me home where I long to be, where I long to be.

附錄 B1

Joy is Like the Rain

I saw raindrops on my window.

Joy is like the rain.

Laughter runs across my pain,

Slips away and comes again.

Joy is like the rain.

I saw raindrops on the river.

Joy is like the rain.

Bit by bit the river grows,

Till at once it overflows.

Joy is like the rain.

I saw cloud upon the mountain.

Joy is like the cloud.

Sometimes silver sometimes grey,

Always sun not far away.

Joy is like the clouds.

I saw Christ in wind and thunder.

Joy is tried by storm.

Christ asleep within my boat,

Whipped by wind yet still afloat.

Joy is tried by storm.

附錄 B2

Time dose not exit in clocks and watches.

God dose not linger in temples and churches.

（鐘錶之內無時間。

廟堂之中無神明。）

附錄 C

Present Past Future

Yesterday is the past.

Tomorrow is the future.

Today is what we have now.

That's why it's called present.

Let's treasure what today offers us.

It's truly a present.

昨天是過去。

明天是未來。

今天是我們現在所擁有的東西。

那就是為什麼它被叫做現在。

讓我們珍惜今天所提供給我們的一切。

那的確是一個禮物。

present 作「現在」解，也作「禮物」解。

昨日已遠飄，明天還未到。今朝是現在，珍惜如瑰寶。

附錄 D

Q: Where does time go?（時間走向何方？）

A: Time comes from the past, flashes through the present and goes into the future.（時間來自過去，閃過現在而通向未來。）

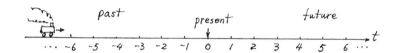

附錄 E

Leap Year　閏年

Thirty days have September,

April June and November.

All the rest have thirty-one,

except February alone.

Which has eight day and a score.

Till leap Year give it one day more.

附錄 F

Ideal, Fame and Profit　理想名利

The ideal symbolizes the sunshine.

The fame symbolizes my shadow.

If I struggle facing the sunshine,

My shadow will always follow me.

But if I turn around chasing my shadow,

I will never be able to surpass it.

理想如日，

名利若影。

迎著陽光奮鬥，

影子總是隨形。

逆著陽光追逐，

永難超越身影。

附錄 G

The Discourse of Great Harmony　禮運大同篇

1. When the great way prevails, the world community is equally shared by all.

   大道之行也，天下為公。

2. The worthy and able are chosen as office holders.

   選賢與能。

3. Mutual confidence is fostered and good neighborliness cultivated.

   講信修睦。

4. Therefore people do not regard only their own parents as parents, nor

do they treat only their own children as children.

故人不獨親其親，不獨子其子。

5. Provision is made for the aged till their death, the adults are given employment, and the young enabled to grow up.

使老有所終，壯有所用，幼有所長。

6. Widows and widowers, orphans, the old and childless as well as the sick and disabled are all well taken care of.

鰥寡孤獨廢疾者皆有所養。

7. Men have their proper roles and women their homes.

男有分，女有歸。

8. While they hate to see wealth lying about on the ground, they do not necessarily keep it for their own use.

貨惡其棄於地也不必藏於己。

9. While they hate not to exert their own effort, they do not necessarily devote it for their own ends.

力惡其不出於身也不必為己。

10. Thus evil scheming is repressed, and robbers, thieves and other lawless elements fail to arise.

是故謀閉而不興，盜竊亂賊而不作。

11. So that outer doors do not have to be shut.

故外戶而不閉。

12. This is called "The Age of Great Harmony".

是謂大同。

附錄 H

單字中 *l* 不發音的字

1. talk [tɔk] *v.* 談話

2. walk [wɔk] *v.* 行走

3. calm [kɑm] *n.* 寧靜；*v.* 使平靜；*adj.* 寧靜

4. palm [pɑm] *n.* 棕櫚樹，手掌

5. Psalms [sɑm] *n.* 讚美詩

6. half [hæf] *n.* 一半

7. calf [kæf] *n.* 小牛

8. could [kud] *aux.* 能（can 的過去式）

9. should [ʃud] *aux.* 應該（shall 的過去式）

10. would [wud] *aux.* 將（will 的過去式）

11. shoulder [`ʃodɚ] *n.* 肩

12. balk [bɔk] *v.* 畏縮不前，猶豫

13. calk [kɔk] *v.* 填塞

14. folk [fok] *n.* 平民百姓

15. palmist [`pɑmɪst] *n.* 看掌相者

16. salmon [`sæmən] *n.* 鮭魚

17. palmistry [`pɑmɪstrɪ] *n.* 掌相術

附錄 I

The Litter Star 小星星

1. Twinkle, twinkle, litter star;

   How I wonder what you are,

   Up above the world so high.

Like a diamond in the sky.

2. When the blazing sun is set,
   And the grass with dew is wet,
   Then you show our little light;
   Twinkle, twinkle all the night.

3. Then, if I were in the dark,
   I would thank you for your spark,
   I could not see which wat to go,
   If you did not twinkle so.

4. And when I am sound asleep,
   Oft you through my window peep;
   For you never shut your eye,
   Till the sun is in the sky.

附錄 J

"UNIVERSITY" may stand for:

"Universally nurturing intellect and virtue with enthusiasm and reason for science, idealism, truth and yourself."

「大學」可詮釋為：

「以熱忱與理性全面陶冶智慧與美德，以追求科學、理想、真理與自我。」

——前教育部高教司余玉照司長

附錄 K

For the want of a nail the horseshoe was lost.

For the want of a horseshoe the horse was lost.

For the want of a horse the rider was lost.

For the want of a rider the battle was lost.

For the want of a battle the kingdom was lost.

And all for the want of a horseshoe–nail.

（少了一根釘子馬蹄鐵不見了。

少了一個馬蹄鐵馬失蹄了。

少了一匹馬騎士輸了。

少了一個騎士戰役輸了。

少了一場戰役王國丟了。

這一切都肇始於一根釘子。）

英文諺語格言100句
One Hundred Proverbs

● 齊 玉 編著

　　本書中諺語格言是由作者利用課餘之暇，從日常生活中慣用的諺語格言裡挑選出來的，大部分諺語後面附有詞彙解釋、音標，並附加文句說明、文法分析，易於理解閱讀。大部份格言諺語都可在三民書局出版之皇冠英漢辭典中找到。相互對照，必能增進對諺語格言之了解。

　　書中所收集之100句諺語格言對讀者英文程度的提升，學習興趣的培養，都有莫大的助益；而對讀者的做人處事甚至人生觀也可發揮啟示作用。閱讀本書，可收一舉兩得（KILL TWO BIRDS WITH ONE STONE.）之功效。

英文成語典故 *Tell Me Why*
—— 解答你對英文慣用語的疑惑

● 李佳琪 編著

　　作者在留美期間，親身體驗台灣人對英文慣用語的陌生和害怕，又見台灣坊間介紹其由來的書籍寥寥無幾，因此成了作者出版此書的動力。

　　此書配合西方的歷史文化背景，以輕鬆幽默的口吻介紹英文慣用語，讓讀者從一則則有趣的故事中，瞭解英文慣用語的由來及用法。